Acclaim for Gloria Emerson's

LOVING GRAHAM GREENE

A *Los Angeles Times Book Review* Best Book
A *Chicago Tribune* Best of Fiction Selection

"A deeply moving tribute to American decency and good-will, with all its frustrations and tragic consequences. . . .
[A] worldly, wry and fond portrait of a zealous do-gooder.
It takes a clever writer to make you laugh at a character
while you feel so much for her too." —*Chicago Tribune*

"Emerson is a forceful and passionate writer. . . . In an age
when moral detachment is so often the rule, it is inspiring
to find a novel that cares so much, and with such grace, for
the failures of its own people." —*Newsday*

"*Loving Graham Greene* is a meditation on the powerless-
ness of those who simply want to do good in the world.
. . . Emerson is too worldly an author not to recognize her
protagonist's naivete (and the novel is full of wry and delightful worldliness), but Molly's fond dreams and painful
disappointments are universal and will be understood by
all decent people." —*The New York Times Book Review*

Gloria Emerson

LOVING GRAHAM GREENE

Gloria Emerson's book *Winners & Losers*, on the Vietnam War and its effects on Americans, won a National Book Award in 1978. She has traveled to El Salvador, Gaza, and Algiers.

LOVING GRAHAM GREENE

LOVING GRAHAM GREENE

a novel

GLORIA EMERSON

ANCHOR BOOKS
A DIVISION OF RANDOM HOUSE, INC.
NEW YORK

FIRST ANCHOR BOOKS EDITION, OCTOBER 2001

Copyright © 2000 by Gloria Emerson

Grateful acknowledgment is made to the following for permission to reprint previously published material:

David Higham Associates: Excerpt from private letters by Graham Greene. Reprinted by permission of David Higham Associates on behalf of the Estate of Graham Greene.

The Independent: Short obituary of Graham Greene from 1991. Reprinted by permission of *The Independent.*

The Library of Congress has cataloged the Random House edition as follows:
Emerson, Gloria.
Loving Graham Greene : a novel / Gloria Emerson.—1st ed.
p.   cm.
ISBN 0-679-46324-0
1. Greene, Graham, 1904—Fiction.
2. Algeria—History—1990—Fiction.   I. Title.
PS3555.M4 L68   2000
813'.54—dc21
99-086033

Anchor ISBN 0-385-72035-1

Book design by Barbara M. Bachman

www.anchorbooks.com

Printed in the United States of America
10   9   8   7   6   5   4   3   2   1

FOR YVONNE

Author's Note

It has been reported that 100,000 Algerians died in the seven years of civil war in Algeria, which ended with the peace plan of President Abdelaziz Bouteflika. It was overwhelmingly approved by voters in 1999. Aside from the great English novelist Graham Greene, all the characters and dialogue and events are products of the author's imagination. Excerpts from Greene's letters come from those he wrote to an American friend. The Algerian novelist and journalist Tahar Djaout, co-founder of a weekly newspaper critical of Muslim fundamentalists, was shot in the head in May 1993.

PART ONE

The frightening postcard from Antibes, with his message written in that tiny, tight English handwriting, said he would not be at home in France when she was planning to visit, for he was going to Switzerland for treatment of anemia. Alas, Graham Greene wrote. Molly Benson knew what anemia meant; an American would have named the disease, but she thought only his close friends would be properly notified. A blood disorder, the family would say. He gave a telephone number for the apartment in Corseaux where he was moving, to be near the hospital, to have the innumerable blood transfusions that he would find so intolerable; but it was two weeks before she managed to call. It was never her habit to ring him; for years, she only used the mail. Her panic grew so acute that she dialed clumsily, reached a wrong number, and was chided by a cantankerous woman, who suspected a wicked prank. Then she was able to reach him. His voice was higher and thinner now, and all that was required of her, she thought, was to make him laugh,

3

hardly one of her gifts. She spoke too rapidly and in a loud voice, although his hearing was very good. It was his eyes that were failing, he said; he could not read. This was unthinkable.

"I wanted you to know that the kiosk from *The Third Man* that Harry Lime used to get down into the sewer," she said, as if medication or pain might have blurred memory of his own great film, "has been re-created in an arcade on Fifty-fifth Street. It looks strange, because it is gilt. It is called Gottfried's and sells magazines and newspapers."

She was certain that he gave a low chuckle, and then provided an end to the conversation, for she would have gone on too long and he had to be careful of this.

"Thank you for calling," Graham Greene said. "And good-bye." It was such a drawn out good-bye, his voice lifting at the end of the word, as if he were leaning out the window of a steam-engine train beginning to pull out and hoped to be heard. It was not yet two in the afternoon, but she could do nothing except rush to bed and pull the quilt over her head, not caring that she still had her clothes and shoes on, wanting it to be very dark, wishing she had sent him her love, although he did not need that from her.

Hours later Molly thought she should fix a drink, something new to her, but there was no gin in the kitchen cupboard, which is what she needed to make a toast in his honor. She stood in front of the three shelves where the work of his lifetime was arranged so carefully, year by year. All the countries where he went for material—Mexico,

Vietnam, Sierra Leone, and the Congo; Cuba, Paraguay, and Argentina; Spain and Panama; Sweden and England. Muddled, Molly remembered that Graham Greene drank gin that afternoon in Antibes, from the bottle of Tanqueray she had bought at the airport as a gift for friends, which she impulsively bestowed on him, to his amusement. She was also, now, in her hour of grief, persuaded that his great and most haunting male characters always drank gin, forgetting that Fowler, among others, in *The Quiet American*, preferred scotch at home in the old Saigon when it belonged to the French, or a beer on the terrace of the Continental. She made her silly toast, something about the talent and generosity of the man, his courage and wit, holding up a mug of tea to the books, and felt no better for it. "To Graham Greene," she said out loud before the weeping began. She could not hear the noise coming from her own throat, which was a harsh gurgle. "His genius and his goodness." She even prayed, back in bed, that he be spared more tubes and needles, the fiddling of nurses, the ring of solemn, neat doctors around his bed, and slide calmly into a coma, curious and happy to finally see what was waiting for him. It made her hiccup, as she had as a child when excited or upset, so she put her face inside a paper bag and took deep breaths.

In Princeton, where she found the weather fickle and sad, no one seemed to know that Greene was dying, and she was grateful for this. Standing before a mailbox in Palmer Square in front of the little post office, Molly Benson raised a stamped letter to her lips and gravely kissed it. There was the sense this was the last letter she would write to Graham Greene, and she felt sick and did not move.

A tall, stout young Englishman, mailing a T-shirt to his sister at home, said: "Is everything all right?" His was a good-humored, ruddy face.

"Yes, yes," Molly said. "Thank you. It is a letter to a friend of mine who is very ill." She did not give a name.

"How sad," said Toby Plunkett, who talked to everyone, everywhere, in a high-pitched voice that told of his pleasure at being abroad. He was like a tap out of which words flowed and could not be turned off.

"Yes."

"Do come and have some coffee. Perhaps you will feel better," said Toby, who had seen her in the little bookstore and thought her aloof. She did not often wait on customers except at Christmas, when people seemed at such a loss, muddled about the titles of books they thought they wanted and suspicious of best-sellers. They were steadied by Molly's firm opinions. That day she needed someone to sweep her away from Palmer Square, which Toby did, and her melancholy did not dent his boyish spirits; he did not need her encouragement to talk about himself. He gobbled two doughnuts with his coffee and she paid, which he seemed to expect.

Graham Greene died at the age of eighty-six in April of that year, 1991. Molly comforted herself by saying that surely he did not want to go on too long, but now her face showed what so many other faces did, the old despairing expression of life.

It was fourteen years since they had met and talked. She knew that he did not easily submit to the earnest and probing questions of journalists, or anyone else, on the modern soul or the religious and political motives in his work. People wanted to find out everything—even if he got down on his knees to pray and if he attended mass. It annoyed him, he said, to hear the word "Greeneland," as if he had invented such a terrain and there was not a real world of barrios and open sewers, of tin shacks and too little food. Molly wanted to ask if Father Rivas in *The Honorary Consul* was in any way inspired by the real Father Camilo Torres, who joined with guerrillas in Colombia and was killed. But she was too timid and, in her happiness at being with him, asked nothing except how Ho Chi Minh, whom Greene had talked to so long ago, might have learned English, as he had noted in an article.

How many times, Molly thought, had Graham Greene accommodated the stranger who had so little to offer and was of less interest than the most minor character he had created.

The huge obituary for Greene was on the front page of *The New York Times* below the fold, and even Molly approved of it.

In New York, Molly's best friend, Bertie Einhorn, was drinking carrot juice for breakfast and talking to her husband about Greene.

"Of course he was a wonderful writer, but the women in his novels were so often prostitutes," said Bertie. "There was that idiot Phuong in *The Quiet American* and Clara in *The Honorary Consul*."

"I think you slightly exaggerate," said Arnold. "I thought Aunt Augusta was hilarious—remember *Travels with My Aunt?* And for God's sake don't make that comment to Molly. She'll be on the phone with you for hours."

"No, she couldn't bear it," said Bertie, who had only read those two novels, although she pretended otherwise.

"And *Our Man in Havana* was hilarious," said Arnold. "He was an extremely funny writer." It was his last word.

Molly was not Greene's only American admirer by any means, but none were held by such a fierce and obsessive attachment as she. "He taught me everything," she would say when people would ask the reason she so loved his novels, and the man as well. It was hardly an answer. She kept on looking in newspapers and magazines for any mention of his name, his novels, the terrain of Greeneland, or tapes from any of the interviews done so long ago. She asked other people to be on the lookout too, but there was rarely a response. Friends did not bother, or want to encourage what they considered a morbid or uninteresting eccentricity. Molly's mother, Diana Benson, would say it was just a little hobby, but knew better. It was Molly's secret that she planned to give a scrapbook to Graham Greene's grandchildren, who would surely cherish it and show to their children, but details of how to bestow such a gift were still vague.

"I can't bear the mail now. There will never again be a letter from him," Molly said to her mother as the year of Greene's death finally came to an end. She could not bother to open any of her thirty-six Christmas cards, putting them in a box on the floor of a closet, behind a jumble of shoes she no longer wore and intended to give away.

"Really, dear, you must pull your socks up," said Mrs. Benson, who was not much of a reader and therefore puzzled by the intensity of her daughter's feelings for a man she had only seen once. It was not becoming behavior. What offended Mrs. Benson, who did not choose to admit it, was Molly's grief for anyone other than her older brother, Harry, who was killed in 1981 in a small, ravaged country where Spanish was spoken. Sometimes she even forgot its name. For ten years the two women never spoke of him, seeing this silence as sacred, as if the mention of his name might somehow vulgarize or diminish the immense, constant loss they felt, a steel lid just above their heads that would never be removed. Once, Molly tried to explain her devotion to Graham Greene to her mother. "He took sides," she said. "He was fearless." No one who heard this, and there were plenty of them, remembered or cared what all the sides once were but he always had. What he found indecent was the injustice that the poor of the world were in the habit of enduring, and the arrogance of the dictators and the bloated malevolent governments, so often propped up and pampered by the United States, especially in Haiti. He protested the war in Vietnam and the fate of the Russian dissidents in the years of their persecution. But he was no more anti-American than many intelligent Americans, Molly would say. She was very fond of some of the American characters in his novels. There were the Lutheran missionary and his sister, of German stock, in *The Power and the Glory,* and there were Mr. and Mrs. Smith from Wisconsin in *The Comedians.* Mr. Smith was a presidential candidate in 1948, running on a vegetarian platform. All of them were courageous, decent, unpretentious, and of helpful disposition. Even Pyle, the ridiculous character in *The Quiet American,* with his puerile ideas on how to save Vietnam, was not cowardly or contemptible. After Pyle was murdered, the British journalist, Fowler, who had a hand in his death, was unable to banish him. Haunted by the American, Fowler wished there existed someone to whom he could say he was sorry, the last words of the novel.

Loving him from the first minute when he stood in the doorway expecting her—she had climbed the stairs, because the elevator would have been too abrupt—Molly understood she would not win his attention. Or not in the way she secretly wanted. Her mother had once been beautiful, but that beauty had blurred and gone slightly askew in her daughter, as if in a careless photograph, and Molly never minded this except for the time she spent with him.

After their drink, Greene suggested that they might meet the next evening, after dinner, to take a walk so he could show her about. Like a child suddenly awarded an undreamed-of prize, Molly felt her face turn pink with pleasure. And so they set out, his pace as fast as her own. He showed her the old ramparts of the port and took her to the place du Safranier. It was a district that was old and working-class and considered itself rather superior to the city, Greene said. There was a dance, and he thought she might enjoy seeing the fun. He led the way down a long stone staircase to a small square that was rather crooked in shape. People were dancing the polka very fast and laughing. There was a bar where everyone stood and men had to shout to make themselves heard. She had never seen the French so jolly and roisterous, believing them to be a cold, combative, and cunning people, clearly not a view shared by Greene. Watching, the two of them were unwatched, of no interest at all. He liked looking at the pretty women who were dancing and admired one blond girl in a red sweater who caught his fancy. She had a splendid carriage and good shoulders, and looking at her, Molly Benson felt a very deep pang of jealousy. If the little band—an accordionist and a trumpeter—had only played a waltz or a fox-trot, she would have asked Greene to dance, but this did not happen. People wanted loud noise and oom-pah-pah.

"If Molly was so devoted, why did she not see him more often?" Posy Stretch asked her friend Diana Benson.

"Mr. Greene traveled a great deal," Mrs. Benson said. "Once he was going to Panama when Molly planned to be in Paris, and another time he was off to Russia. He had a house in Capri, too."

In her misery after his death, Molly Benson decided to lead a little delegation to Algiers in the hope of rescuing a few writers there, in Graham Greene's honor. A New York committee advised her, by mail and by telephone, that a growing number of Islamic fundamentalists there were threatening writers and journalists opposed to them. The committee only wanted money, but Molly thought she might locate a few doomed men and pay for their tickets to leave the country. This was a chance, too, to see the great colonial city the French had embraced for 132 years and relinquished in chaos and disgrace.

It seemed a sensible, laudable plan to her. Other people, when asked by Molly, thought it was berserk but said nothing, for they knew she would not listen to their misgivings. It was puzzling to them that a wealthy woman in her forties would live like a penitent, in their eyes, and deprive herself of so much to give away money in such a haphazard and useless way. It was not apparent to them that Molly held to a plan to help those who had no hope at all of being helped, but others saw the entire Third World as the Last World, whose numbers were too vast, whose languages were unimportant, and whose diseases were too abundant. It was a different matter if there were game parks or rain forests to visit. Molly wanted to do more than write checks and go to board meetings, understanding that if she did things on her own, only a handful of people might be assisted. The trips abroad were not always productive. Peru, for example, had been a failure. But a few successes deluded her into believing she held to a moral code.

Her last trip was to Lagos, Nigeria, an asylum of a city, to inspect a children's clinic whose work was praised by a medical group in Seattle trying to raise funds for it. In Lagos, it was by chance that Molly learned of a playwright who had been imprisoned, although not for his plays. He was not famous; no New York group had taken up his case. The incarcerated man had refused to pay a bribe to his landlord, who had relatives on the police force. A nurse in the children's clinic, where the small patients made so little noise, told Molly about the man, who was her brother. It was easy enough to provide a little help and bribe a guard. It was another story with the sick children; the easiest ones to help had only skin diseases. She pledged ten thousand dollars and appointed the nurse, an Ibo, to be head of a watchdog committee to make sure the funds were not wasted or embezzled. Bertie Einhorn thought it a most successful trip, and Molly was pleased, too.

Only Arnold Einhorn, Bertie's husband, refused to see it.

"The money Molly spent on the tickets and the hotel would have kept ten families alive for five years," said Arnold, who liked to declare that Molly wanted to be poor herself and that it would be her only success. Now she thought this might be the last trip, for the expenses were great and she recognized a degree of self-indulgence at work. But it was the traveling she loved, the purposeful journey, the mission at hand. The trips eased a peculiar sense of placelessness. Driven behavior, an unqualified psychologist told Molly's mother at a dinner party.

Algiers was waiting. In that beautiful, shabby city, two religious men in their late fifties, genuine penitents, were talking about small things after their dinner, cooked as always by the smaller, thinner one, with the sweet smile, Lucien. The dishes had been washed, dried, and put away by the noisier, needier man, Eugène. A plate was chipped and another cracked, so special care was taken. They could not be replaced. Nothing could, for both men had long ago taken a vow of poverty.

"Did you hear that noise last night? The rat-tat-a-tat? I was unable to go back to sleep," Eugène said. But Lucien, who was brushing up crumbs and wiping the coffee table, shook his head and said no.

"A policeman shooting at a bat, or perhaps a rat, for diversion," Lucien answered. He knew what had to be kept from Eugène, who was prone to panic and whose nasty, fanciful premonitions kept on blossoming. Since Lucien slept so soundly, he never heard noises at night except for the frolicking of mice in the living room, where he slept. But Eugène was not so lucky and never admitted when he had eight hours of deep, uninterrupted sleep, for he believed every night was splintered by unearthly noises.

In time, Diana Benson learned of her daughter's plan to go to Algiers and take that witless New York friend with her. Another mission of mercy, Mrs. Benson would say, mouth pursed, but it was she who cleared the path. The Frenchman who cut her hair in New York for special occasions was married to a woman whose brother was a priest of some sort in Algiers and might be of help. Pierre affected great joy at seeing Mrs. Benson in the salon, as if a dear old friend who needed his help had returned at last. He favored older women of her ilk; they did not whine like fretful children and tell him they felt dehydrated or exhausted, that their necks hurt and their new diets were killing them, that their highlights were too dull or too brassy. Pierre talked as he worked, and she bent her long, thin neck far forward as if in rapt prayer while he cut the back. Upright, Mrs. Benson came to the point, mentioned Molly's plan to go to Algiers and how grateful she would be for any help and guidance, saying that Molly would call Pierre and, of course, write to the brother-in-law well before arriving. As a measure of her gratitude, she immediately bestowed a nicely folded one-hundred-dollar bill. "It is too good of you to help," Mrs. Benson said, with her famous smile, which still made men want to be obliging.

"And how are Molly and her husband?" said Pierre, who had four women, waiting with wet hair, in various stages of sulking and dejection. He had once thought of going to Japan to do the models' hair in an international fashion show and Molly's husband had been mentioned as someone who could show him around.

"Molly is well, and Paul is still making that film in Japan. One hardly asks for details, or why it is not finished."

Pierre was always grateful that her bulletins were so brief, and that night he spoke to his wife about Molly's plans. Marie-Claire had never been to Algiers to visit her brother, since her distaste for Algerians was corrosive, but she knew that Lucien and his friend Eugène could easily put up Molly and her friend. They lived in a house provided by their religious order, and there was space for guests on the top floor.

"I've only seen the daughter once. She has hair like a horse—and so badly cut. She came to the salon to pick up her mother wearing a man's old wool bathrobe over a mink coat. She had chopped off the fur sleeves," Pierre said. Mrs. Benson, in fact, had been deeply agitated at the get-up, since she had given Molly the mink coat years before—but not to wear under her brother's old bathrobe. She thought her daughter looked like a madwoman.

"That could be very chic," said Marie-Claire. "I'll write to Lucien. Their lives must be so boring. Maybe it will be exciting for them, something different."

Since she never read a newspaper or watched the news on television, Marie-Claire was quite unaware that the two men feared great trouble coming closer and did not want excitement of any kind. Lucien never wrote of political turmoil in his letters to her, which barely filled a page.

"Ask the daughter if she will take a package for them—it's the least she can do," Marie-Claire said, who wrote to her brother in Algiers the next day.

Eugène preferred to let his fears and sorrows build up before he aired them at length to Lucien, expecting that an accumulation would have more impact on his old friend. He was sitting meekly, ankles crossed, hands clasped, waiting for Lucien to come home from the hospital, which was always at four-forty-five in the afternoon. Perfectly still,

Eugène managed to fill the living room with a small turbulence.

"I have lost three pupils. Their families are going to France. The fathers sent me notes to say so," he said. "They said they were worried about the situation here, which they consider very unstable. Two of the fathers mentioned FIS." He used the acronym for the party of the Islamic fundamentalists. Then his round face puckered and he sang out in anger as if pronouncing a curse: "Le Front Islamique du Salut."

"But, my dear Eugène, FIS was started in 1989 and is outlawed and we have had no reason to be worried now," said Lucien. "We are not in danger." He looked in the cupboard for some chocolate that his mother had sent him from France and found two squares left in an old jar. It was very stale, but it had a calming effect on his friend, who munched the little pieces like a child. He wanted chocolate the way some men craved a drink.

Far away, in her dusty Princeton apartment, Molly was writing to Lucien how happy she would be to stay with her friends in the house in Algiers and said that details of their arrival would follow. It was one of her bad days, so Molly wrote in English, which Lucien was unable to read, and did not know anyone who might translate. Molly was deeply distracted sorting out the Greene obituaries, including a packet sent by her friend Polly Wiggins in London. For the last fourteen years of Graham Greene's life, it was Molly who cut out and sent him all articles of interest and even reviews of his new books, which the publisher sometimes neglected to send. She found his address in France quite musical: La Résidence des Fleurs, rue Pasteur, 07710 Antibes. The little building where he had a three-room apartment was not as grand as the address: On the balconies, other tenants grilled food when the weather was warm, and the odor of cooked meat infuriated Greene. Brief letters from him always came to Princeton typed on a single sheet of white paper with an engraved address in small black letters. Once, he was especially pleased to have her "cuttings," as he called them. They were the obituaries of Kim Philby, his old friend from the British Secret Service, the master spy who defected to Moscow in 1963, where he lived happily for years, much to the horror of those in Britain and Washington, D.C., who wished for him a life of remorse and pain; humiliation, at the very least. Greene thought that the American obituaries were more moderate than those of the British press. He had never turned against the marked man, understanding the power of Philby's belief and the price such faith demanded.

I t was always in honor of Graham Greene, who would have been faintly amused if not encouraging, that Molly carried out various subversive misdemeanors which not even her mother would have thought possible. Inspiration for this one was a photograph from El Salvador that punctured her heart. Two young women, faces in the earth, hands bound behind their backs, lay lifeless, propped up on the high embankment of the main highway to the airport in San Salvador. Their shoes were missing.

"Oh God, the poor little things, the poor little things," Molly said, slithering into a rage. "The death squads again." She wanted to protest, but had only the feeblest idea of how to avenge the deaths of the two and honor them at the same time.

Bertie Einhorn, who needed to be steered into trouble, was always willing once the first bare outline of an idea was flung at her. No friend was more fiercely loyal, although others did not know why. Bertie and Molly were an unlikely pair. Schoolmates while growing up in Princeton, the two little girls had loved each other instantly, so much so that they started their own detective agency. "We'll Do the Job Fast" was the slogan on the little hand-lettered cards they passed out. Bertie was living with her grandmother, while, in New York, her parents pounded out their divorce and lied about their assets and all else. It was the grandmother who hired the girls to find a pair of missing eyeglasses, which meant searching eight rooms in her house. Mr. Benson asked the children to track down a book on the Battle of the Bulge in his library because all the World War II titles were jumbled.

"It would be lovely to humiliate the ambassador from El Salvador during one of his dinner parties by putting cement in all the toilets, but that's too ambitious a plan," Molly said. "So we'll frighten an official in the city." It was easy enough to find the name of the consul general and the address of the consulate. Molly called and said, in an officious voice, this was Flowers by Igor with a delivery for Señor Hector Rodriguez from Elliott Abrams, an assistant secretary of state who backed the war and did not denounce the death squads.

The receptionist was not impressed. Molly asked if such a large arrangement of flowers should be delivered to the office or to Señor Rodriguez's home at 510 Park Avenue. It was an old trick that her brother Harry had taught her: Give the wrong address, and people will automatically provide the correct one.

"It's not Park Avenue," the receptionist said. "Señor Rodriguez lives at Waterside Plaza, apartment 9B."

"Delivery Tuesday from Flowers by Igor," said Molly. It was startling to be such an accomplished liar, she thought, and useful. She hired the nineteen-year-old son of a friend of her mother's to drive into New York when the plan became crystal-clear. She would carry an immense bouquet of flowers to the man's apartment. The mission was to deface his front door with handprints in white paint, to scare the consul general to death. He would tell his superiors, his family, and his friends. "Mano Blanco," said Molly, remembering a bright red door with huge white hands on it, paint dripping. It was how the death squads in El Salvador announced that an assassination had been carried out in the house. "Gloves won't work. You dip in your left hand and I'll use my right hand," said Molly. Bertie was to buy turpentine and bring a rag so that they could clean up in the car. It was Bertie who knew the terrain, for she had once left a shopping bag at the office of her dentist—who was capping her perfect little front teeth—and had been obliged to fetch it that evening at his apartment.

"It's a ghastly complex. Four huge buildings on the East River. There are thirty-seven floors in each building and at least ten apartments to a floor. A car lets you off at street level, but the doorman is on the plaza level on the third floor. We won't have to be buzzed in if we wait for someone to come out. We're in luck." She always said that when she was nervous.

It was on the appointed Tuesday that they embarked. The affable boy at the wheel, who wanted an extra bit of cash, took Molly to the worst florist in Princeton, drove into the city, picked up Bertie, and listened to the drumming of her instructions. "Go across Twenty-third Street, sharp turn to the left, and let us out. Here, here! Don't leave the car. Wait right here for us."

Two Vietnamese, leaving for the United Nations by car, held the door open and Molly gave them a radiant smile. The flowers almost concealed her face: Pussy willows and orange sunflowers, which she detested, came to her nose. The long-stemmed roses had begun to droop, as they usually did, and even the tulips and freesias looked fatigued. She was used to the flowers cut from her mother's garden, where there were two huge white lilac bushes.

The building was so somber that people walking down the dreary brick hall to the elevators knew where costs had been cut by the builders. The walls were a dull tan and the carpet an unfortunate brown. Bertie carried a heavy can of white paint and a flat screwdriver in case the lid did not easily come off. Outside the steel door of 9B—painted a cream color, which was a disappointment for Molly, who had hoped for a red or dark blue—they went to work. Molly was the first to put a hand in the paint and press it hard against the door. Then it was Bertie's turn and she made a little face. Molly thought four handprints were enough. When they were finished, she saw that the door simply looked as if it had been decorated by capricious children, that even a dim-witted man might not be taken aback. Their hands were too narrow, but Bertie said there was no time to improve or enlarge, so they fled, leaving the flowers on the floor near the incinerator.

It was Bertie who provided the gloves to cover their hands. "No one was home," she said to the boy snoozing in the car, as if it needed an explanation, as if he cared what they were up to. The smell of paint was strong, but he was not a curious type. Both women, although crestfallen that their handprints did not look more sinister on the door, felt like commandos; they were elated and spent. Molly was thinking of the two girls lying on their stomachs until people who loved them would carry them off. Rigor mortis would come in eight to ten hours.

"Of course the consul general only handles commercial interests, he doesn't make policy," Molly said, discovering that Bertie's glove would not come off her right hand. The paint had made it stick to the skin. "But he makes it possible, humoring the banks who make loans to businessmen in El Salvador. And they probably pay the death squads while the U.S. pays everyone else."

Bertie thought they should leave marks on the doors of the banks who were guilty and do it in a dawn raid.

"They wouldn't know what 'Mano Blanco' means," said Molly, but the idea had such charm that they talked about it for some months before the death of Harry blotted out the world.

That night, Molly wrote to her husband about her day. Paul was in Osaka making a film about two lovers working in a pharmaceutical factory who were organizing a strike.

"I know most people would think me ridiculous, but I don't care," she wrote. "There have been so many deaths in that country that no one will fuss about these two unimportant girls, so I had to do something. However small and mean. I hope they haunt their killers. Maybe it is true what G.G. once wrote: 'The dead have more value than the living, they have more power, they may answer your prayers.' "

The trouble was that Molly Benson did not pray and, in any case, would never ask anything for herself, believing that millions had more urgent requests and needs. She envied Graham Greene the years of his great faith and tried to picture the very tall, thin man at a 6:45 A.M. mass in Vietnam, where, he wrote, it was strange and moving, in the big cathedral, to be the only European. She did not know anyone who was devout. Christianity can survive without Europe, he had written forty years ago, and without America too, she thought.

A hint of religious belief was lodged deep within her, but she never felt it stir or grow. Paul, her husband, was a

Buddhist and affected immense calm and optimism, even during the endless trials of making the film. He wrote cheerfully of various setbacks, quite forgetting that she did not know the names of the Japanese crew or cast: "Umi has an abscessed tooth, so filming has been delayed," or, "We are doing more casting since I have written three new characters who will be important," or, "Toshiko had an automobile accident in our van and some equipment has been damaged." She thought he was not coming back for some time, that the film was a Tolstoyan epic which would eat him up, that his close friends working with him—whom she would never meet and whose names were Yoshi, Hiroko, and Cheiko—would serve out their sentence as willingly as her husband and believe that it counted for something immense. She became accustomed to his absence, as might the wife of a man at sea, and the vacancy in her life was not caused by Paul as much as by the loss of her brother and Graham Greene. Molly's missing men, Bertie thought. From Japan, Paul sent a flood of staunch and bright predictions: "We have some really brilliant footage. Even the director, who is never pleased, is now pleased. Hold on."

She found it easy enough to sit it out in Princeton, where she had grown up, and almost loved its beautiful blankness and horrible damp summers, which the well traveled compared to their old sufferings. India always came to mind, so relentless was the humidity despite the healthy splendor of large trees everywhere. She like seeing the students, who wished ardently for higher grades, for great praise, for love and freedom.

Even in misery they were compelling, because their faces often shone with distress. You could overhear them in the Annex, where students went to eat, although their meals at the eating clubs were paid for in advance. They yearned to travel, but Molly could not feign interest in the ruins of Turkey and Mexico. She wanted something else: to get medicines and all sorts of help to the Kurds, to Cuba, to Romania, to Cambodia, to Chad, to the Sudan, to drug addicts in the Bronx. The list was a roll call of devastation and was not to grow smaller.

In New York, her stockbroker would say to his assistant when Molly would occasionally call for money to be sent her: "She's pissing away her capital." It was not the case, but he hated selling Merck or GM to help some orphans in China or in Peru. It was torture for him to hear her reasons for wanting funds, but she always gave them, as if to punish him for his profession. Her account was far too large for reproach on his part.

She did not like money or trust its power. Her inheritance made her feel uneasy in a country where the poor were so easily humiliated and seen as morally inferior. There was always the need to distance herself from a culture she abhorred, a society deformed and contaminated by money, sickening itself, insatiable and pathetic. No one could repudiate this except by abnegation, by sharing, and by a strict refusal to consume or to yield to any frivolity.

"Of course, Molly doesn't have children or it would be a different story," some friends liked to say, and were right.

Her mother, who hoped Molly would overcome her unnatural tendencies, gave her pieces of her own jewelry, since that is what mothers in Princeton tended to do when they grew old. But there was no hope for such a daughter.

A gold bracelet went to Bertie Einhorn, who felt rapture looking at her wrist; a small diamond clip went to Bailey Fleming, who was divorced and without alimony or work; and a strand of nice pearls went to Harry's childhood friend Annie Cross, who wept over lunch in New York when presented with it because Harry was now dead. "I should have worn them at our wedding," she said. "We were coming to that, you know. Certainly by next year." Annie, who had loved Harry when they played tennis at the age of fifteen, went on and on, unable to eat her shrimp, her salad, a torn roll. Molly slid into shock and could only stare at this woman, whom she considered a numbskull, with her beige hair and tanned skin, the slightly uneven eyes welling up. It turned out that Annie went to dinner with her brother in Mexico City not once but twice, that old feelings had bubbled up, and that Harry and she had laughed so much, as happy people do. In Molly's mind, the woman was delusional at the very least.

"It was wonderful. And he made me wait in the lobby of some hotel, a rather nasty little place, with an envelope stuffed with dollars," Annie said. "I had very strict instructions. I was only to hand it over to a man who said: 'Señora, are you hungry?' in Spanish. It was quite thrilling but nerve-racking. The fellow was twenty minutes late." The money for the guerrilla hospitals, Molly thought.

Harry had used this idiot to carry out her wishes, and then she too began to cry, so the food on her plate turned into pools. He did it for me; this is what I wanted, she told herself.

"We are family now," said Annie in a final, exaggerated embrace.

Annie soon realized that Molly was not listening to her.

What a cold fish she is, Annie thought. Why doesn't she wear makeup? No one would pay her the slightest attention if it weren't for her money. And she doesn't even have a job, just that dinky foundation of hers.

It was eight years since Molly's wedding to Paul, which Annie attended because Harry was best man. The groom, it seemed, was without family or many friends. Two of them, rather scruffy men in borrowed blazers, who had gone to film school with Paul in Berkeley, seemed unable to explain what they were now doing. Annie, and others as well, found it a strange wedding, with Molly and Paul listless and dutiful, as though the house on Lilac Lane were a huge hospital room where guests had to be humored as cranky patients might, the cake eaten like medicine, the rituals meekly observed so health could be restored. Molly's mother grew wildly vivacious as the pall thickened. Some of the older guests, with Posy Stretch leading the way, voiced their surprise at being asked not to send wedding presents but rather contribute to the Southern Poverty Law Center or Madre, which helped women and children in Central America. Checks were to go to Molly at Lilac Lane. "Rather off-putting," said Mrs. Stretch. "Of course, it's customary to be asked not to send flowers to a funeral service and to contribute to a charity in the name of the deceased, but at a wedding . . ." She sent a nineteenth-century English soup tureen anyway. Only two checks arrived, totaling one hundred and ten dollars, and one donor even phoned Mrs. Benson to ask if her contribution was tax deductible. What came were two sets of candlesticks, several lead-crystal bowls, silver frames, Italian pottery, salad plates, fish plates, champagne glasses, and assorted vases, which Molly donated to Trinity Church for its annual rummage sale.

Long after the wedding, people remembered Harry and spoke of him. Molly complained to Bertie. "People make up these little stories about the dead as if to magnify their own importance in those lives," she said. "It's an awful form of deceit."

"I'm mailing you a wonderful blue cardigan," said Bertie.

Only she could give Molly the occasional present, because it was always secondhand: a sweater or a vest or a jacket, things that other women had once liked and now found wanting or wrong.

It was un-American, Harry would always say of his sister; there was a mutant gene at work. It was their last afternoon together, only six months before his death, and he lightly touched her hand as they talked about the revolutions in Central America, thinking she looked quite pretty. Molly wanted Harry to take money for the crude field hospitals run by the guerrillas in their zones in El Salvador, an illegal and treacherous act in the eyes of her government. He thought it might have to be done through the representatives of the Farabundo Marti National Liberation Front in Mexico, a tricky business; but he promised to try.

The house was cold, because Mrs. Benson believed heat was the enemy of wood and her antiques would be warped if it was warm, so Harry went to his old room, filled with books and possessions of his boyhood, to look for a sweater. He came back with a tattered paperback of Graham Greene's essays, which he had read and heavily marked in college.

"The virtues of disloyalty," he said. "Ah, here it is. Greene wrote, 'Loyalty confines you to accepted opinions. . . . If we enlarge the bounds of sympathy in our readers, we succeed in making the work of the State a degree more difficult. That is a genuine duty we owe to society, to be a piece of grit in the State machinery.' "

"I just give away bits of money," said Molly. On the death of their father, Harry turned over his share of the inheritance to Molly's little foundation.

"You treat money as a penance and you manage to disturb so many people. We'll be grits together," he said. They beamed at each other, and knew the luxury of sitting for a little while in happy silence.

What upset people, of course, was not that she gave away money but that she needed so little for herself, and seemed to want nothing.

There were Harry's presents from Central America in

her lap: an embroidered blouse and a woven bag. There was the very light straw hat with the high crown and huge brim that she put on and would have worn at dinner if Mrs. Benson had not playfully wagged her finger and said: "Now, now, no sombreros in this dining room."

The ordinary hat, worn by the poorest of men, always hung from a nail in her living room, the first thing she saw on entering her apartment. There was a pale trace of dust on the immense brim; all over Princeton people were complaining about the heavy traffic on Nassau Street, which bestowed grime everywhere, and how shocking it was to see so many trucks. What was admirable was the view from the front windows: the imperial FitzRandolph Gate with the eagles on top of massive columns, their heads turned toward each other; the trees and the lawn that kept so many men employed in tending them; and Nassau Hall, with its names of the war dead lettered in gold on marble walls in the front hall.

Molly called her little apartment "the office" and had a student working three days a week. Elsie Blodgett sorted mail, checked three newspapers, filed, and ran errands. There was no reply yet from Algiers, since Lucien had put off writing her in the hope that she had changed her mind about the trip. Eugène's indigestion was now troublesome.

"Good news," said Elsie, holding up a story from *The Washington Post* when Molly came back to the apartment. It was on the personalities of the Supreme Court justices, which were not apparent in oral arguments or in their writings. She always liked to read aloud any passage about Greene from the press; it was the nicest part of the job of sorting the mail and cutting and filing the papers for Molly three afternoons a week. She began: " 'Obviously displeased with the government's policy of summarily returning Haitians who flee their homeland, Blackmun' "—Elsie stopped to explain that his full name was Harry A.—" 'asked a Justice Department lawyer, "Have you ever been to Haiti?" "No, your honor, I'm sorry, I have not." He then asked, "Are you familiar with a book called *The Comedians* by Graham Greene?" "No, your honor, I'm sorry, I'm not." Justice Blackmun responded: "I recommend it to you." ' "

It did not matter in the least that Elsie spoke with a lisp so the reading was slurred; Molly stood very still, her thin face made younger, rearranged by joy. The novel had been published in 1963 and a justice still remembered it. It was hard to believe that such men ever read novels.

There was a note with the story from a retired CBS correspondent in Maryland who had known her brother in Central America and was faithful in sending clips to Molly. "It means so much to her," said the CBS man before he walked to the nearest mailbox to post the letter, but his ill-tempered wife thought it might be more sensible if Molly paid for a clipping service, since she could easily afford it. All this fussing, she went on, as if Graham Greene were out of print. The sweet man, wishing for the old days when he was on his own in Greeneland, as he always thought of it, only put on an extra stamp on the packet, since the post office was so unreliable. "No hope for Haiti," he wrote Molly.

"Things only seem to get worse there. Mathilde and I are well and hope you are busy doing all the good things you want to accomplish." The note went immediately into Molly's files, which also held an earlier letter from the same man when he had left CBS. The legs and the wind have gone, he would say cheerfully to friends but in fact, the network had not picked up his contract, wanting younger faces at lower salaries. Seven overseas bureaus had been phased out. He no longer watched the evening news on television; it seemed ridiculous to him. His letter was a reminiscence of a happy day in London when he first saw Graham Greene.

"It was 1975 or 1976, because I remember puffing myself up to ask the great man a question about the fall of Saigon. I remember that he was tall and slightly stooped, wearing a very good old tweed jacket and a pair of half glasses, which made him look awfully severe. My impression was of a man thoroughly distinguished and deeply pained. The Foreign Correspondents' Club in London was prestigious in a stodgy sort of way. But I was surprised he had agreed to talk to us. There was no small talk, no witticisms, no attempt to win the sympathy of the audience. He read from a prepared text and he spoke of nothing but Haiti. He was making an appeal for the correspondents of the world to pay some attention to a place that was being totally ignored. His delivery was earnest and untheatrical. I had never seen this group of Americans, always pretending to be British, so completely cowed before. Prince Charles had lunched with us previously, and while everyone toadied to him, this was different. Greene wasted his time, of course. Haiti was off the map then and was to remain so for a long time."

He never wavered or backed down, Molly thought, or felt himself too important to be bothered.

Elsie was in charge of assembling a file on the troubles in Algeria and, because she was only nineteen years old, was startled by the grisly murders. She put off calling the airlines about fares, since there was no rush.

The trip to Algiers was being delayed, since people invited to join the delegation were stalling; the short war in the Persian Gulf, although over, made them fearful of traveling. At the suggestion of Posy Stretch, who had friends in the English department at the university, Molly looked up an assistant professor who taught Jane Austen and spoke French perfectly. Molly pursued the young scholar for weeks, until he finally admitted to her that his family was opposed to the trip. They were having coffee on campus.

"My grandmother is Jewish, you see," he said softly. "She would not want me to go to an Arab country with Islamic guerrillas." He began to droop in the heat of Molly's glare.

"It's North Africa, not Iraq," she said. His grandmother happened to be a Lutheran, but he lied to escape Molly's clutches.

It was this disappointing defection that suddenly made Toby Plunkett a possible recruit. On a Thursday in the bookstore, when Molly was sorting out an order of books, Toby came charging in to look at a new biography of Field Marshall Sir Bernard Montgomery. She drew him aside and said: "Toby, I need you." He was thunderstruck; no one ever seemed to need him. After hearing a summary of the reasons for the trip to Algeria, he felt himself anointed, seized Molly's hand, and babbled his acceptance. Work on his dissertation would tie him up for a few months, he said, but then he would take a break and go anywhere with her. To seal their pact, she gave him a paperback copy of Greene's *The Comedians*.

"Of course I've read it, but how nice to have another copy," Toby said. "A remarkable novel." This seemed a good omen.

Elsie Blodgett was done sorting the mail when Molly returned home, having put the appeals in a bulging red folder. The file on Algeria was now more ominous in its thickness. Elsie took off, making the usual racket in her lumberjack boots as she raced down the little stairs, the backpack in one hand scraping the wall.

The apartment had four irregularly shaped rooms, none large, with bookcases that rose to low ceilings and seemed to tilt. Some of the furniture, inherited pieces, was quite nice—a Trumeau mirror, four Hitchcock chairs, a blue and white Chinese rug in need of cleaning—but the occasional visitor was never audacious enough to say how charming it was or what pretty rooms, because there was a haphazardness to them, an indifference. No one tidied up. The small dining room was where the two women worked, on a refectory table that was never polished.

Elsie felt slightly triumphant on that day, for she had stolen twenty dollars from Molly and once more was getting away with it. But Molly knew and had left the two ten-dollar bills on a table, half under a vase, as if by careless-ness, so Elsie was spared having to forage for it. Molly used to have a cash box, which was without a lock, but Elsie rif-fled it and took larger sums. Since Elsie was the one who was sent to the bank on Nassau Street to cash checks, she handled a good deal of money over time. Once Molly no-ticed a discrepancy of one hundred dollars and asked Elsie about it, peering into her wide, dreaming face.

"The teller probably made a mistake, and I didn't have time to count the bills because I had so many errands to do," said Elsie, in the accommodating tone of an overworked servant. She expected to be found out and, now that the cash box was not in use, picked up what she found lying about the apartment.

"I don't think she actually needs the money," said Molly on the telephone to Bertie Einhorn. "Her family must be poor—there is that to consider. Once, she told me her di-vorced mother, who has two young children, married a man with three children who live with them. The house is so crowded that when Elsie goes home on a break, she has to study in the bathroom. She lies in the bathtub."

"It must be very uncomfortable," said Bertie.

"She puts pillows and quilts in the tub," said Molly.

So she and Elsie had their secret pact, for Molly was will-ing to lose small sums every week. She thought that even if she gave Elsie a raise, Elsie would still need to go on steal-ing. Her good intentions did not win favor with the stu-dent, who was waiting for a scene that never came. Elsie despised such well-meaning people and thought they deserved to be cheated, or punished in some way, because they were rich fools. She was unrelenting in her opposition to benevolence.

Molly went to work: The personal letters, always put in a blue folder by Elsie, included one from London, from the notorious Polly Wiggins, who was late in sending a page from the *Independent* magazine. Readers had been invited to write the obituary that Graham Greene might have written for himself. It was the weekly writing competition. A bottle of champagne went to the man who had written:

> "What sort of a fellow was he, then?" asked Sir John as the coffin was lowered into the sodden earth.
>
> "Who? Greene?" said Dr. Percival vaguely. "Writer chappie, I believe. Never read any of his stuff myself."
>
> "Was it anything like Conrad? I like Conrad, though I can't say I care much for the modern writers."
>
> "Well, perhaps. He was our man in West Africa once, you know. Quite pally with Kim out there. Caused a bit of a stink."
>
> "Was he? Do you know, I had no idea Conrad was one of ours—he must have been tremendously old at the time, mustn't he?"
>
> "No, no: not Conrad; Greene. Chap whose funeral this is."

"Ah, I see. Sorry." Sir John surveyed the church-yard gloomily. "Catholic, of course?"

"More or less; bit bolshie, I'm told. But then we're all bad Catholics nowadays, aren't we?"

"Yes. Yes, I suppose we are."

It did not amuse her: He and Philby were not together in Sierra Leone. Greene was in MI6, in the British colony, 1942–43, and used Freetown, the little capital with its tin roofs and vultures, as the setting for *The Heart of the Matter*. It was the novel he grew to most dislike, Greene told Molly that day in Antibes, for people misunderstood it. He had written this as well.

What was on Polly Wiggins's mind was the Balkans and the negotiator for the European Community, who, she felt, had legitimized the seizure by the Serbs of Bosnia and the slaughter of Muslims. Her own husband could no longer bear to hear her on this subject, so frequent were her outbursts. She wrote that if Molly wished to make a trip to Sarajevo with some medical supplies, she was on the alert and would gladly go with her, no matter the peril. But Molly knew it was impossible for them to get a seat on a U.N. plane going to Sarajevo. Only journalists and those with a large accredited relief organization qualified. After two pages of vitriolic condemnation of the British government, Polly returned to her favorite crusade: to change the names of two streets in the city of Bristol, which had played a major part in the slave trade in the late seventeenth and eighteenth centuries, shipping Africans to American plantations. The streets were Whiteladies Road and Blackboy Hill. Polly wrote: "We can't move the local M.P. or the city council, and the local press couldn't care less. People say, 'Well, that's all in the past, no reason to change names now.' " Even the BBC, which had an office on Whiteladies Road, was indifferent to the complaints and petitions of Polly's committee. It drove her mad.

There was a muddy spot on the letter, as if Polly's huge and insipid dog, named Tooter, had placed his paw there as some sort of message. It was always a source of distress to Polly that in two novels Greene had written acerbically about dogs. Only Molly remembered them: In *The Quiet American*, Pyle's dog was a black chow with a black tongue, who was named Duke; and in *The Human Factor*, Castle's dog, with his bulging and hypnotic eyes, was Buller, who had to be shot when his owner defected to Moscow.

Before her was the pile of appeals, sixteen of them, and two letters thanking her for donations made. There were seven invitations to join committees. There was a wrenching appeal for a group trying to send aid to the Sudan and a note from a nun, Sister Madeleine, in El Salvador, who ran a feeding station for children under ten and gave some food and milk to about three hundred a day. She wrote for help on very thin, yellowing paper that did not match the envelope.

In Algiers, the manager of the great El Djazair Hotel, with its three hundred rooms, its marble floors, its richly tiled walls, its nightclub, its swimming pool, its splendid restaurant, felt a cluster headache coming on. Two waiters had not shown up for their shift at lunch, three bellboys were no longer on the premises, and he was uncertain why. The concierge said they could all be replaced, but then it was his job to placate people.

"What is going on?" said the manager, quite roughly.

"Perhaps the buses have broken down again and they are afraid of being so late," the concierge said. But he knew better and suspected that the missing men had been warned by FIS not to work at the hotel, which put up so many foreigners. It begins, he thought.

So many countries jostled for attention in the crammed little room where Molly worked, and this is what occupied her. There were photographs on one entire wall: the enlarged snapshot she had taken of Graham Greene in the armchair in his small living room, holding a drink of gin in one hand, behind him a teak table with shelves used as the bar and the bookcases to the ceiling without an inch of space. The man in her picture was grinning as he watched her work the little camera so ineptly, and even Molly knew she was a humorous sight taking photographs. On that splendid day when the camera was put down—he did not much like being photographed—and both had drinks, Molly confided that of all his novels, her favorite was *The Honorary Consul*, and he thought that at one time it might have been his, too.

She knew a passage almost by heart: "Doctor Plarr was a good listener. He had been trained to listen. Most of his middle-class patients were accustomed to spend at least ten minutes explaining a simple attack of flu. It was only in the barrio of the poor that he ever encountered suffering in silence, suffering which had no vocabulary to explain a degree of pain, its position or its nature. In those huts of mud or tin where the patient often lay without covering on the dirt floor he had to make his own interpretation from a shiver of the skin or a nervous shift of the eyes." She had begun to recite it for him in his living room in Antibes and stopped, fearing he might think her a fanatic or so overwrought that she would fling herself in his arms, which is exactly what she most wanted to do. Before they parted, Molly heard him say of the new novel to be published: "Perhaps this time I've gone a bit too far." It was *The Human Factor,* and she gave it to everyone at Christmas, including her mother, who would have preferred the usual gift of Guerlain soap.

There was the Black Star photograph on her wall, too, of Greene in French Indochina in 1951 talking to two French soldiers, in helmets and camouflage, long scarves around their necks. Greene, so much taller, was laughing at the jokes of the man with the binoculars, hands in his pockets. There were a few mementos from Harry's little apartment on East Seventy-fifth Street, where she used to go, if notice came before he came back from one of his grueling trips, to make sure there was food in the refrigerator, that the rooms were aired, the mail sorted, the place fluffed up, since Molly suspected the cleaning woman might not care, which was true. Harry was away so much that the tired woman was nonchalant by now, as if she were taking care of a modest tomb. So Molly lined wastepaper baskets, bought rolls of paper towels her brother would not use, fruit he would not eat, cookies he did not like, a new shower curtain he would not see, cleaned windowsills and dusted, although he would not notice. There was a photograph in his living room that Harry treasured, taken by Sebastião Salgado, of two boys in a mountain village in Ecuador. They were sitting on a tree trunk in front of huge cacti, their hands together, thumbs touching. In soiled clothes and funny little school caps, the children were extremely solemn, as if the camera were bestowing an unusual privilege and dignity was needed. It was an unspeakably sad photograph, and their faces and hands were dirty. She believed them to be brothers. They were the children of a world that Graham Greene once knew so well in Mexico, the Congo, Cuba, Paraguay, Argentina, and Nicaragua, so it was fitting that in her apartment the photograph was put next to the one of him.

That night, as usual, there was nothing at home to eat but a tin of sardines, which she made into a sandwich with leaves of old lettuce. Once again she did not bother to go to the supermarket, as if groceries would magically appear: Buying and cooking food were tiresome, and she would often go to Y. Y. Doodles on Nassau Street for noodles and beef. Because she did not own a car it was necessary to walk to Davidson's supermarket and buy only as much as she could carry in her backpack. "Like a soldier," Harry used to say, laughing. He thought it was hilarious to look inside her empty refrigerator, with its old jars of different mustards and jams. "Stop snooping," Molly would say, but she had been guilty of this, too.

She had spied on Graham Greene that afternoon in Antibes, because she wanted to see everything of his. On the pretext of getting a glass of water in the small, unused kitchen, she opened the door to the refrigerator. A woman had fixed a plate for him with a few slices of cold meat and cheese and a tiny salad, which might have been for his supper. It was strangely moving. There was no other food, not even fruit. Except for the books and a little Haitian painting, the apartment had a pleasant anonymity. It was without framed photographs, mementos, magazines, tributes, or plants, as though even a cheerful or comforting clutter might distract him from writing every morning, those five hundred words a day. There was the house in Capri and a Paris apartment, but Molly never thought about them. He sometimes wrote about food he had once enjoyed, but did not want the bother of buying and cooking it—exactly how Molly felt, although cooking was now a required passion in her country. People talked about different kinds of lettuce and mushrooms, about hams and cheeses, as if to prove how cultivated they were.

Once, in Princeton, her mother saw Molly walking home slowly—she had a quart of water in one hand, another in her backpack—and was startled by the sight of this tall, shabby woman in old sneakers, her gait made crooked by such weight. Mrs. Benson planned to speak to Molly, but Posy Stretch was driving them to the reading group and it was late enough. She knew full well that people like her did not count for much anymore except with each other and were without influence or power, since their imperial era was gone for good. All they still possessed was impeccable taste—or that is what Diana Benson believed. And you could not buy taste, she liked to say. It made it so aggravating that Molly was indifferent to possessions, to her own appearance, to the maintenance of what she owned, to her bearing. The treaty with her daughter was of such complexity that both now could not remember its provisions, only that they should speak of nothing of import or criticize one another—all for Harry's sake, as if that were the homage due the dead man. Mrs. Benson was aware that this was not considered healthy by other Americans, but she thought it suitable conduct for those of her upbringing, who did not babble about their feelings to strangers or to family. Brief complaints over the years to close friends were different, and it was understood, although not explored, that Mrs. Benson did not really like her daughter, and knew regret.

It was Harry, of course, who had charmed and delighted her.

She did not fully understand, or choose to, that her son was dead until his postcards stopped coming and for some months found herself on the lookout, so the mail—if it could be called that, since human letters were lacking—

became a torment. The catalogs came by the pound, page after page of clothes or objects she thought ugly or vulgar. The fund-raising letters—HELP US it said on one envelope, in scarlet—seemed intrusive and futile. She would not respond and had all of it thrown away, every week. Only Molly studied the mail, a traveler inspecting a map, and even ordered an inexpensive summer skirt from one catalog to send to Sister Madeleine of the feeding station in El Salvador, who was astonished. She was unaccustomed to nice surprises.

In Princeton, the mail almost never came before noon, so burdened were the letter carriers, but in Algiers it was delivered midmorning, for the postmen were not weighted down with such terrible and unwanted loads. The two men received almost nothing. Eugène had no family or friends, and for Lucien there was only an occasional handwritten letter from his aged mother, asking him once again to return to France so she might see more of him in her last years on earth, last months perhaps. It was a forlorn song she had hurled at him over many years, the tune never changing. She detested the Algerians but pretended otherwise.

"If you are so attached to these people, there are plenty of them who need you in Paris, in Toulouse, in Marseille," the mother wrote. "They are poor. No one likes them." She never stopped praying for him, the mother wrote, forgetting that so long ago it was she who had shoved him into the order and the sweet boy had obeyed, and found happiness.

But now on a Tuesday came a letter from his sister in New York, who rarely wrote, on thick, cream-colored paper, the envelope festooned with bright stamps that said LOVE. She had put on twice as many as needed, uncertain of the postage. Marie-Claire always had a tendency to be wasteful, but living in America had probably aggravated this shortcoming, Lucien thought, making her profligate.

It said: Pierre has a charming client whose daughter plans to come to visit Algiers with two friends, the reasons not clear, but their visit would be short and how much nicer for them if they could stay with Lucien and Eugène rather than in a hotel, where they would be overcharged by Arabs and perhaps treated badly. (She was thinking of Saudi Arabia, where foreign women, uncovered, without a male relative, were unwelcome.) Were there enough sheets and towels? She would call him shortly and send, air express, anything that was needed. The very idea shocked Lucien, for of course there were extra sheets, old, but nicely mended by French nuns some years ago, before they were sent back to France and hated having to go. The rooms would have to be dusted, but nothing could be done about the old brown stains in the sink.

He put the letter on the table in the living room, where he always slept on the couch, a habit even though there were beds he could claim, and know comfort. He shared his mail.

"Americans?" said Eugène. They did not have secrets from each other, and his alarm first showed itself in the manner in which he sucked in his lips and rubbed one side of his forehead as if to forestall a headache. "What do they want?" he asked. Eugène was found deficient and unreliable, if not silly, by the elderly, retired French cardinal, who presided over nothing but had once held great power. It was the wish of the cardinal, who had stayed on after independence, that he be assigned to the care of Lucien, knowing that a lesser man could not tolerate this but that this patient man would. *"Vous faites encore des bêtises?"* said the sharp-tongued old cardinal when he saw Eugène in the mansion that was still his, on a hill. Eugène looked too honored and was genuflecting before the great old relic, a pantomime of piety at best. *Are you still doing stupid things?* Eugène flushed deeply and was hurt; there were so few of them left, he thought he might be greeted more warmly. He and Lucien had arrived in 1964, two years after the end of the war, and never found it necessary to learn Arabic, so deep was France's imprint, so profoundly had the colonial power insinuated itself into the psyche of Algerians. Lucien worked, without salary of course, in the El Salam Hospital, but Eugène stayed home, unfit for the world of work, giving lessons in French to the children of professionals who wanted their children taught by Europeans so they could qualify for universities in France. But Algerians were not so welcome now, since the troubles, and all were suspect, so France was shutting them out. There was still a scattering of French priests in Algiers who taught poor children in the slums or worked with the severely disabled or labored in important ways. Not so these two.

Their order gave each man a monthly stipend so small that Pierre, the hairstylist in New York, would have been offended if in one hour his tips were not far larger. Extreme frugality kept Lucien in good spirits, and in a schoolchild's notebook he kept tidy accounts, which no one would ever want to see.

He was so humble and patient, so gaunt, that this small man with thick gray hair, the texture of a toothbrush, offended no one, and even inspired spurts of generosity among some merchants. In the big open market where Lucien, who did all the cooking, shopped for dinner each weekday at 4 P.M., when he was done at the hospital, the butcher sold him the cheapest cuts of meat. Sometimes he put in an extra piece of mutton or lamb and did not charge; Lucien smiled at him. "Not like those other French sons of bitches," the butcher said to his wife. He told people he had killed at least six French soldiers at close range during the war. But the woman did not like any European, thin or fat, and would have yelled and carried on if she knew of the little gifts of meat.

"There was trouble last night, another journalist shot," said the butcher to Lucien that week, but the European did not seem to hear; he and Eugène did not discuss politics or the growing disorder, for they thought this unseemly and were poorly informed by choice.

Eugène kept an eye out for the mailman, because the foreigners were coming, and a slight panic pushed him to the gate to see if there were letters. Usually, any mail was left in an open box hung on the outside of the large pale villa in the old compound for foreign priests and nuns. There were only five left, the remnants of a sovereign power whose influence was negligible. Lucien and Eugène were a little distance away from the villa, a downhill walk on old stones, a turn to the right, and then a row of three houses facing a field where, once, vegetables and flowers were grown in the old days. That day, detesting the exercise, Eugène walked to the high green gate, never locked during the day, to see the postman approaching at his usual hour, talking to himself. He was happy to see Eugène, but anyone would have been fine and he drew him to one side and insisted on whispering.

"You cannot believe it—the police held me yesterday for four hours," the distraught man said. "And such questions! They lasted forever, it seemed. They wanted to know about what kind of mail I delivered in the neighborhood and whether any of it might be from the Islamistes—you know, propaganda or notices of meetings from FIS. As if I read the mail I delivered, and I told them so! They were quite rough with me, very impatient. And they told me now I would have to be more alert and look at envelopes because from time to time they would want to talk to me."

Eugène put his hand on the man's shoulder to steady him, for it was the least he could do. He managed to look distressed, for he was quite good at that. On the veranda a Polish nun watched and then went inside, where there was always work to do. And it was the three nuns who cleaned the little church that you first saw looking through the bars of the gate. It was a severe church, small and painted the wrong shade of beige, too pointed and plain, the cross on top slightly too large. It had been built in the 1930s, when there was a need.

Eugène did not know that he was shuffling as he made his way back to the house, where nothing was waiting for him. It was a bright, forgiving day, but he took the weather for granted and began to sing a child's song in his dry, flat voice to push down the first gush of fear that the mailman had stirred up. He was accustomed to being a coward.

It was the fears that men struggled to conceal which was the subject that night of a forlorn telephone conversation between Bertie and Molly, who spoke to each other every other day. The subject of scorn was once more Bertie's husband, a tax expert. Bertie was explaining, at some length, that his profession had strangled the inner man and killed all spontaneity and wit in poor squashed Arnold.

"He must be afraid of seeming foolish," Bertie said. "He hates surprises or change. It's quite pitiful. Oh, they're all alike." Molly was hoping to explain her new strategy for Algiers: The best way to help any journalist or writer there was to provide the funds for them to hire a bodyguard of their own. But she did not elaborate, since Bertie was busy fretting.

"Have you told Arnold we are going?" Molly said, suspecting the worst.

Bertie was braced for a tiff. It took place, as always, in their kitchen, with its costly white oak cabinets, its huge counter, the stove and two perfect ovens, the floor of handmade tiles from Italy, the eight skillets for different purposes, the alphabetized spices, the pots with copper bottoms, which Arnold cleaned himself, trusting no one else to do it, least of all Bertie. Only here was he immune from worry or any spasm of chagrin. He was such an accomplished cook that clients and friends often called him at home for help with recipes. "What does it mean to cut on the bias?" asked one client. "Against the grain of the meat," Arnold said. "What is a generous splash of vinegar?" his dermatologist needed to know. "Two to four tablespoons," Arnold told him.

"I think Molly and I will be going to Algiers," said Bertie, setting the table. "But not right away." Arnold was preoccupied with a leg of lamb and a yogurt sauce. No expression crossed his face. In his line of work, people were always peering at him as if the slightest change of expression might be a signal of leniency, the lifting of eyebrows a portent.

"Well of course you are," he said. "Why wouldn't Molly take you to a country having a little civil war? It sounds like a splendid idea to me, a most useful trip." The yogurt sauce did not look quite right, so he was more sarcastic than usual, although he was often critical of Bertie's "liberation mode" of thinking: exploiters and exploited, a holdover from the sixties, which contaminated her in later years. He did not choose to admit that in the case of Algeria, it was hard to know who was doing what to whom and of little interest. The French should still be in charge, he thought.

"Molly is paying for the trip," Bertie added.

"Well of course she is. She had a considerable inheritance—not a huge one, of course, but very healthy—and is using it very rapidly, as far as I can see, on these little crusades or for dubious left-wing causes. May I ask whatever came of your trip to—was it Nigeria? And China? *Nada, nunca, niente. Rien!*" He kept on, for the yogurt sauce now looked more promising. His was once a fine voice, an instrument of splendor. During their courtship, Bertie would keep him on the telephone as long as possible, admiring its timbre, but a sinus infection had done its cruel work.

A prudent man, Arnold was not about to dredge up his huge grievance against Molly—that she had ruined his wedding—and how it forever bound her to the mast. And the subject of Harry Benson's death once set his wife raging when he needed to eat his dinner in harmony. Slaughtered, Bertie would say, as if correspondents were not killed all the time in war zones, as if Harry Benson never knew the risks of working in El Salvador and how treacherous that highway in Usulután was in 1981, when the whole country was a madhouse. Bertie wove these foreign names he did not choose to know into her lamentations: killed by troops that our own government trained and equipped, and the M-16 bullet inside Harry was proof of *that*, Bertie kept saying, but after ten years the outrage sank to a deep, hidden place and she would not discuss it. There was a huge framed photograph of Harry Benson in the living room, and invariably people would ask: "Who's that?" She refused to explain.

Arnold was unable to visualize his wife being effective in any Third World country, lacking, as she did, authority and a commanding presence. He had seen her in the Antigua airport and was not impressed. He thought that before they met, her life had been a series of helter-skelter episodes, dictated by the political convulsions of others, who urged her to commit antisocial if not felonious acts. He had married her in the belief that he would stabilize her, as he put it. In his eyes, Molly was in even worse shape and, since her husband, who claimed to be a Buddhist, was still making that asinine film in Japan, was beyond salvation.

Bertie, with his encouragement and financial planning, now owned a shop on East Eighty-fourth Street, which sold very expensive European clothing, worn once or twice, called Deuxième Fois. Customers were seen by appointment only, no checks were permitted, no riffling through soiled piles of used clothing scattered on tables. From a silver rack hung three or four items—a suit, a dress, a jacket—and more clothes were only brought out from the back when a customer made clear what she was looking for.

The old Bertie had loved being a hooligan who in the early 1970s poured an entire bottle of the perfume Cabochard—already opened—over a policeman who lifted his arm to whack her during a demonstration in Washington, D.C., against the president. She rejoiced in the man's immediate shock at his own smell, his chest soaked by Mme. Gres's great perfume; he was now destined for days of humiliation, because dry cleaning could not entirely lift the fragrance. She was certain he would be ridiculed and scorned by other police officers.

The story charmed Harry Benson, who made her tell it

twice and held Bertie in his arms while he congratulated her. He was back from Vietnam and resting at home for a week with a fever of unknown origin.

"Other women can start pouring their Chanel, their Joy, their Estée Lauder in a new kind of uprising," Harry said, kissing Bertie, who was turning pink with pleasure as his long, perfect hand ruffled her hennaed hair. She had always fancied him, loved the beaky face with the long nose, the eyes that were a bit too close together, the small smile, the voice.

In Harry's messy room in the Camino Real, after his death, Molly and Bertie had sorted everything and were startled by an unfinished letter written in French, on hotel stationery. "Darling, you are always with me in places you will never see but where the suffering, although different from your own, would not be new to you . . ." Molly was never to know what woman was waiting for Harry to write. In Princeton, there was a commotion about his death and too many questions, as if a plausible explanation of the circumstances might take the edge off it. That year, 1981, El Salvador was in the news, but no one was following closely, so the death of one of their own brought family and relatives to a dead stop. "How could this happen to us?" asked a cousin who came to stay with Mrs. Benson in the house on Lilac Lane, and proved a nuisance. Molly remembered what Graham Greene wrote in *The Heart of the Matter* after Scobie's suicide, when the priest Father Rank thought: "Oh, the conversations that go on in a house after a death, the turnings over, the discussions, the questions, the demands—

so much noise round the edge of silence." The *Princeton Packet* and *Town Topics*, the local newspapers, ran obituaries, which Mrs. Benson would not look at.

It was Molly who found a new way to comfort herself, a tiny crack in the iron circle of sorrow, by deciding, or rather inventing, the last few minutes of Harry's life. He was getting out of his rented car when shot at, from about thirty feet, by a government soldier waiting for him—this much was known. It was in retaliation for the five thousand dollars for the field hospitals of the Farabundo Marti National Liberation Front in the zones they held. The man who took money from Annie Cross in the hotel lobby in Mexico City was an informer who knew the password: "Señora, are you hungry?" San Salvador was infested with informers called *las orejas,* or "the ears," and perhaps in Mexico City, all Salvadorans with links to the Frente in their country were watched and spied on as well. The truth is that Harry had asked Annie Cross to deliver the money because he had an appointment—the silly woman told Molly as much—and that Harry had explained the little errand in a noisy restaurant, where no one could possibly overhear. It was a ludicrous scenario but a version of the catastrophe that bestowed some solace. It meant that Harry died for a reason, a purpose, because he had taken sides and was to be punished for it, although the ignorant, ill-trained, stupid soldier who fired his weapon was never to tell who had given the orders.

It was a different story for Mrs. Benson, who knew no such solace and was to wonder too many times if Harry had lain, still alive, in pain on that disgusting road before being discovered. She could see him in the living room on his last visit, lounging on the white couch, its great pillows puffed so high that it seemed a shame to sit on them. He preferred it to the Chippendale couch in ivory damask that was always admired. Nothing ever changed here: The walls were the palest green, the matching lined curtains had borders of the thinnest lavender stripe, there were the dark portraits of pale, dour ancestors with long, thin noses—Harry inherited this—and small eyes, and polished silver boxes and picture frames and a big white armchair where men usually sat.

"How did you find Molly?" his mother would ask.

"Very fit and busy," Harry said in a paternal manner, waiting for the barrage to start.

"I do worry about her. People see her as rather—well, odd," Mrs. Benson said. She was aware that Molly hated the house on Lilac Lane, especially the living room, with the pictures of those censorious, mean faces on the walls. It was built on rot, Molly thought, on the pursuit of money; beneath the pretty things was a black slime.

She poured tea for Harry and went on about Molly's wasting money, believing that it would never be used up, about the sin of touching capital, about her fixation on that man Graham Greene, who, Mrs. Benson had heard, was called a Catholic writer.

"Molly should have been born a Catholic," Harry said. "She could join the Catholic Worker movement, one of Dorothy Day's children who takes a vow of poverty." He wanted a nap.

"What a dreadful thing to say," her mother said. A last huge effort was required of him.

"Loving Graham Greene makes her want to see a world different from the one she knows, and find out new things about people," said Harry. "That isn't such a bad thing, is it? And actually, I think you could call Greene a Catholic agnostic."

"Posy Stretch's daughter is a stockbroker, and Ellie Lambert's daughter runs a catering company called—what is it now?—oh yes, Yum Yum," Mrs. Benson said.

"Molly doesn't want to buy or sell, to compete in the marketplace. She wants to keep a distance from all that," he said, quite sleepy now.

"The money that Molly is pouring away was made in the nasty marketplace by your great-grandfather in Titusville, Pennsylvania, piping oil. How fortuitous for all of us that he did not feel himself above the fray."

Harry was looking at the television set, in a corner so no one could conveniently watch it, and remembered how Molly at the age of twelve would sit in front of it watching the war in Vietnam. That year it was he who gave her a copy of Greene's *The Quiet American*.

Mrs. Benson had more to say, and pointed out that the Princeton public library had been obliged to refuse Molly's gift of four thousand dollars in exchange for a season of readings from Greene's novels, chosen by her, which would be open to the public. Posy Stretch said they had never heard of such a thing.

"Well, she did meet Greene—yes, yes, by mistake, in

that restaurant in Antibes when he dropped something on the floor and she ran after him to give it back." It made him smile to think of the famous Englishman being pursued by his sister, who was a good runner. Harry knew that Greene, who liked women, must have been charmed by the long-legged American, with her wild hair and huge, serious eyes, who was elated to be facing him. He might even have thought her charming. At any rate, it had been decent of him to invite her to his apartment the next day for a drink.

Her last words on the subject of Molly were not new, for Mrs. Benson had always believed that ceaseless repetition would prove her right in any discussion. Men grew sedated listening to her. But Diana Benson liked to review things, as she put it, as if she were sorting out invitations and seeing what complications lay ahead.

"Even as a child Molly had this peculiar tendency to give things away—her dolls, my old fur jacket to the cook when her husband was run over, the jade bracelet your dear aunt gave her, her allowance in college to that Mexican room-mate, and now her inheritance. It would cause your father great worry."

By now Harry had earned his nap and went off, and Mrs. Benson cooked the roast beef for dinner herself, since it was his favorite.

"It's rather comforting to have children who are so devoted to each other," she said on the telephone the next day to a friend, and for once meant it.

Only Arnold Einhorn remained detached after the death of Harry, although he did spend hours making a cassoulet—

her brother's favorite French dish—when Molly came to dinner. He thought of Harry as a marginal journalist at best, another freelancer gorging on disaster. Two weeks before their wedding, Bertie had suddenly been conscripted to go to El Salvador with Molly to bring the corpse of Harry Benson home: Her dear friend could not go alone. Once back, Bertie was in a fugue, telling him over and over between spasms of sobbing how Molly was certain that the corpse of her brother, lying in the cheap casket with its odious white rayon lining, was not clean and that there was dust inside his mouth and in his hair. She had made Bertie fetch a damp washcloth from the hotel so she could sponge his face and mouth, and it was so shocking that a priest visiting the funeral home had tried to stop her; the dead man was clean enough. Harry's chest wound was hidden. On her return, Bertie needed sleeping pills.

The small wedding was spoiled, Arnold thought, the atmosphere macabre—two pale women heavily made up as if that might conceal their shock, grimacing at the guests because they didn't seem to remember how to smile. It was bad luck that Molly was maid of honor, although he had to admit she did her best to hold up, while Bertie looked like a woman who had been led to the gallows and suddenly let go.

He knew everything about the death except a dreadful slur against Harry, which neither woman could ever bear to bring up again. After the brief little service, which two dozen of the press corps attended—quite used to it by now, for more than six of their own had been killed, with the A.P.

man saying how Harry would be missed—Molly and Bertie were invited to dinner by the correspondent for *The Wall Street Journal*. His face was kind and tired. All of them were in the Camino Real Hotel, where the clerks at the front desk were worked to death and had their favorite guests, preferring the television correspondents, who flew in and out and needed at least four rooms for their entourage and scattered large tips about.

It was quite by chance that Molly and Bertie were ten minutes early when they appeared at the room of the *Wall Street Journal* man, fifth floor, the door left open. Molly needed a second before they plunged in, took a deep breath, and then froze in the hall.

"He was a very decent fellow," said the *Wall Street Journal* man, who was shaving in the bathroom and talking to someone sitting on the bed. "We had some good times together.

"The trouble is that you couldn't quite trust what he wrote," he went on, his voice loud above the electric razor. "That story about the young woman guerrilla in Chalatenango was a little hokey. Slightly too perfect. And that story from Morazon—well, it doesn't matter now." The *Wall Street Journal* man had read Benson's stories during his last trip to New York; he always liked to see what others were filing.

"No, it is not important now," said the other man, sadly. Molly, standing very still in the door, thought he worked for National Public Radio. It was a young voice with good diction. Exeter vowels, Harry called it.

"The hell of it is that you don't have to make anything up—it's all so grisly and awful. And his Spanish was good enough so that he could have played it straight."

"Yes," said the radio reporter. "But he didn't deserve what happened."

"He is the third person killed on some bloody road. It could have happened to any of us," said the other man, now rinsing his face and splashing on his Dior aftershave for dinner.

"Oh God."

"The sister seems to be holding up well," said the other man, as if he should be credited for this. Then Bertie coughed and Molly knocked and entered the room, but neither of the journalists was clever enough to see that it was anger, not grief, that was now changing them and was most visible in the way they held themselves.

The *Wall Street Journal* man steered the two women like tottering invalids to the hotel dining room, past the tables of journalists, who stood up when Molly came into sight and gave brief mumbled condolences in the manner of men, suddenly made shy, who know their duty. It was Bertie who did the talking, who thanked people who came over to the table for their kindness, and who even chose what she and Molly would eat from the elaborate menu. Molly was too busy imagining Harry living in the hotel, having fish for dinner at this very table, checking for messages at the desk, meeting people in front of the theatrical little fountain in the lobby, so she was good for very little.

There were intrepid young women in the large press

corps, mostly photographers who kept their camera bags with them at all times, even when they ate. All of them, their hair cropped or worn in a long braid, seemed to have skin dried from the sun and nice handshakes. One of them, the size of a twelve-year-old, with tiny wrists and ankles, sloping from the weight of the camera bag on her left shoulder, came to Molly's room on the day of departure, when most of Harry's clothes had been given away—the helpful *Wall Street Journal* man, again, taking them off to a mission—and Molly had nothing left to do but observe the various forms that her own suffering could take.

"Hi, I'm Puffin," the woman said, as if last names among Americans were irrelevant here.

"I'm sure Harry told you about our plans to open a photo gallery in New York," Puffin said, not noticing that Molly's stare was blank. "It meant so much to have this plan. We both felt we had cratered out in Salvador."

"Cratered out," said Molly, up to her old trick of repeating what she could not comprehend.

"He planned to take Rosa with us, of course. He would never leave her behind. And I've come to ask if you might have a keepsake I could give her—a little thing of Harry's—because she is too upset to meet you."

"A keepsake," said Molly, her speech shredded.

"She was so good for him. She even found some old woman, a healer, who worked on his scalp for those awful headaches he had. We used to joke about this smelly salve she put on him."

"His headaches?" said Molly, jolted, hearing her own

breath rise and fall. In her handbag, which held the letter in French to another woman he had loved, she found Harry's beautiful Cartier watch, which she so wanted for herself, and gave it to Puffin, saying that their father had given it to Harry before his death and he had always worn it. Puffin was grateful, said so, and promised to send a photograph of Rosa, as if the grieving sister had a shrine in mind and needed a lineup of women who loved Harry.

A long time later, walking down Nassau Street on her way to Woolworth's with Elsie, she was to see the watch for the last time. It gleamed on the wrist of a poor man, short, with huge shoulders, dark-skinned, and slightly bowed in the legs. Molly ran after him, shouting in Spanish for him to stop, which only made the man run faster down a side street until Elsie grabbed her arm and yanked her to a halt.

"He's a Guatemalan—probably a dishwasher at La-hiere's," Elsie said. "There are lots of them in Princeton. You almost scared him to death." Molly knew the man was Salvadoran, knew he smiled at her as they passed as if a secret trembled between them, and knew that perhaps Rosa had given, or sold, Harry's watch to him, or that it had been stolen from her. But Molly was never to know the smallest detail.

In New York, Arnold was putting his foot down and asking Bertie for her full attention. It was not hers to give, for that week she had witnessed a dreadful scene and could not concentrate on very much, making work at Deuxième Fois out of the question. Looking out the huge living room windows of their apartment on Central Park West, when the early-morning light seemed the palest green and the reservoir almost reminded her of a lake she had once loved in Europe, she saw an assault on a man walking a white dog on a long leash. In a swift and savage ballet, he was suddenly kneed in the back by an assailant in orange shorts and, falling backward, was garroted, all in a minute or so. The dog was kicked and went berserk. People in the elevator, leaving for their offices, could hear Bertie's dreadful shrieks as they passed her floor. "Don't interfere, Phyllis," a man said to his wife, who wanted Oscar, the elevator man, to take them into the Einhorn apartment to offer assistance. The woman thought a man was battering his wife, but in the street the husband told her: "It's too early for that."

Arnold was solicitous but nevertheless needed to voice his insistence that a reliable person—preferably a man, since Algeria was an Arab country, not the bastion of Presbyterianism that Molly seemed to think—accompany the two women on their trip. Without a man, they would be scorned or detained, as if they were off to Iran or Saudi Arabia.

"She's already found someone," said Bertie. "His name is Toby Plunkett. Molly says he is very chatty. He's thrilled to go—free trip. He's an English historian who likes Tintin and speaks some French."

Arnold was placated. Another novelist and a newspaper editor had been shot that month in Algeria by the fundamentalists, according to a small story from a wire service in the *Times*. The same week in Princeton Molly took Toby Plunkett with her to see an old film, *Battle of Algiers*, being shown on campus to a class of film students. The 1965 Gillo Pontecorvo masterpiece reenacted a chapter of the fighting in the Casbah between the French paratroopers and the Algerian resistance. Molly told Bertie not to come, because she thought her friend would not hold up well after her recent ordeal. The opening scene of the film showed an Algerian coming out of torture, bent with pain and shock, barely able to shuffle or swallow. The affability of the French who had gone to work on him and were relieved the job was now done only made worse the shame and self-loathing of the victim, for he had told them what mattered. Toby Plunkett blew his nose loudly on two occasions with a soiled handkerchief, which seemed to Molly, whose own face was wet, a very good sign. Outside, in the winter dark, his thick ginger-colored curls seemed to grow wilder in his distress. His presence was so required on the trip that Molly chose not to notice some revolting habits—how he sucked in his spaghetti, his head bent low over the plate, when she took him for dinner at the Annex, the cheap restaurant.

When it was clear that Toby intended to analyze the film in gruesome detail, Molly waylaid him by talking about a letter from Graham Greene years ago in which he had written that there were two politicians in the world whom he detested: Ronald Reagan and Pope John Paul. Toby, who had opinions on everything, thought the animus toward the pope was deserved, because he had thwarted the Liberation

Theology movement in Latin America, suspecting it of being Communist-inspired.

"I'm still rather hungry," said Toby. "Let's have dessert." It was her first clue that he required immense amounts of food, and she remembered, with an effort, the chaste plate in Greene's refrigerator and that he had written that his weight was usually 180 pounds, not more. She only ordered pie for herself so she would not have to watch Toby scrape his plate and lick the fork. He had already wadded up two paper napkins and was working on a third.

Professor Harvey Chalk, of the committee called Aid to Writers and Artists Abroad, called Molly from Vassar to suggest some men in Algiers she might help. One hunted man was a prominent writer who only wrote in French, was unable to leave his house, and sent occasional pieces to a local newspaper by a twelve-year-old courier who came at night to take them from his garden, where they were put in a designated bush. However, the professor's own favorite writer was Tahar Djaout, author of *The Bone Seekers*, on whom he had written a paper.

"The narrator is from a Kabylia village in the mountains who after the war of independence is over sets out to find the remains of his brother," Professor Chalk said, but was gently cut off by Molly, who thought he might be starting the same lecture he gave to his class in Literature of the Other World.

"You will have letters from Arabs in this country that can be gotten to the extremists through middlemen, and I am sending you the name of their lawyer, Monsieur Yacef." Professor Chalk was not sure if Molly's idea of hiring bodyguards would work, since they might turn out to be suspicious characters, but maybe the priests could find local men with weapons.

"It's not dangerous right now, but move about as quietly as possible and make known the worry in this country," he said. As if a Muslim fanatic would care, Molly thought.

Most of the writers and intellectuals were against the fundamentalists, or "Islamistes," the professor said. The difficulty was that the Islamic Salvation Front had recently won a national election by fair means but was told by the government that it was not allowed to win, and the results canceled. It was preposterous. The government of the National Liberation Front was corrupt and inept, while lower oil prices had shattered the economy.

"They have been negligent for many years and have grown stupid and lazy," Professor Chalk said, sighing.

"Do you think we can be of some use?" Molly asked, worried about a wrong turn.

But the professor, who had been drifting, suddenly came to a halt. "A million Algerians died in the war with the French, and now they hunt each other," he said.

She began reading Tahar Djaout's *The Bone Seekers,* which Professor Chalk sent her, along with his good wishes for the trip. It was in French—printed by Editions du Seuil in Paris and never translated into English. At first she read it aloud, but this slowed her down and she knew her accent was abominable. The novelist had done his studies in mathematics and was a poet and journalist. The story was unspeakably sad: The young narrator eventually finds the remains of his brother, but understands how futile it is to have done so—his village needs the bones of its dead not only to honor them but to shield themselves from a changing world. The villagers are smothered by too many dead, and to go on living they must change in the deepest, most difficult ways.

She would take *The Bone Seekers* with her to Algiers for the author to sign. It wouldn't be hard to find his address.

There was a huge box from Marie-Claire and Pierre to take to Lucien and Eugène, which she could hardly lift. It held a jar of jelly beans—which Pierre found amusing, since President Reagan so loved them—four tins of shaving cream, a jar of peanut butter, which Lucien would never have tasted, six tins of Norwegian sardines, a box of chocolates, and many articles of clothing.

"If you see any of those nice woven little prayer rugs, bring one or two back if it isn't too much trouble," said Mrs. Benson, thinking ahead to Christmas.

The abscess in Lucien's molar, lower right jaw, flared up again, making it impossible for him to chew, so he considered going to a dentist but did not. He knew the dentist would demand that he have work done on nearly all his teeth, and the expense would be impossible. It was not the pain he feared. Eugène, who for many years had worn dentures, insisted that if he rubbed whiskey on the inflamed gum it would help, remembering how his mother, a French farm woman, had done this for him when he was a boy facing decades of toothaches. He thought in those years that everyone else had treacherous teeth. But there was no whiskey in the house, and to buy an entire bottle was shocking to them.

Eugène, who was more cunning, then asked one of his most prosperous pupils, whose worldly father did not abide by the Muslim prohibition on alcohol, to ask him if some whiskey might be donated. He gave her an empty jar, once filled with olives and saved, as everything was. For medicinal purposes, Eugène kept saying, tell Papa this. When the obliging child returned with his olive jar almost filled, Eugène went to his room and took a swig. He felt a strange rush of rapture and began to sing to himself. Lucien, suspicious of this manic mood, rubbed some whiskey on his inflamed gum and poured the rest down the old porcelain kitchen sink. It surprised him that the unpleasant smell lingered a day or two. He did not know that Eugène had saved some whiskey in his bathroom glass and hid it under the bed for solace for when the foreign visitors came. He planned to have Lucien say that he was in the grip of a migraine headache and must lie still in his bed, curtains drawn. But well before Molly Benson and her companions arrived, he had finished it off, waiting for more noises in the night coming at him like death squads.

"In a few days they will be here," said Eugène to Lucien morosely as they finished their little dinner of dolma, a zucchini-like vegetable stuffed with meats and onions. They ate in the living room on a small, low table; Lucien cooked, making just enough for the two of them. Neither man was accustomed to large meals. Lucien was growing thinner and Eugène stouter on the same amount of food. Their visitor that night was a twenty-year-old university student, the daughter of Algerian doctors, who was a pupil of Eugène, who taught philosophy, logic, and grammar at home, although not an educated man himself despite his airs. Lucien was sweeping the indoor stone flight of stairs that led to a heavy front door while Eugène was once more drying the dishes. The pupil, Hediya, turned on their tiny black-and-white television set and groaned. There was only one state-owned channel, and she was obliged to watch *Battle of Algiers*, which she had grown to loathe. Repetition had done the impossible and made the great film boring. She was being dragged back to the Casbah.

"Oh, not again. Why do they keep putting it on? We've all seen it hundreds of times, day and night," said Hediya.

"Now, now, stop that," said Eugène, folding the old dish towel. He used a spare bedroom as his office, where he sat at a desk and looked sternly at the poor work of his pupils. With her coat now off, Hediya was all legs, because of a short skirt and the black mesh stockings her mother had purchased for her on her last trip to Paris to see a gynecologist. In Algiers, doctors did not have good equipment and lab work was inferior to that done by the French, she said.

The stockings, the wisp of a leather skirt, were to wear at home or when Hediya had friends over, but in public the clever girl concealed it all under a long black coat her mother had found in a Left Bank boutique. Women did not prance around in Algiers in a brazen way, but no female ever had to shroud herself in black, although older women sometimes covered part of their faces with little white squares of cloth.

It was all changing for the worse. Hediya was nagged so persistently by her mother about the furies of the fundamentalists that she even covered her hair while driving her parents' car so the bogeymen would not see her and thrash her as her mother predicted.

"She doesn't see what's coming," Hediya's mother said to her husband. They spoke to each other in French.

"We must live between resignation and despair," said the doctor, an ophthalmologist, who had read his Camus.

Hediya swaggered around in her black coat, which came below the ankles, acting like a desperado.

"I wish I could live in France," she said to Eugène, who was looking at her composition and correcting sentences in purple ink.

"No one would understand you, since your subjective is confused," he said, but softly, because Hediya was his favorite and he heard a plea for leniency in her voice. He knew full well that the girl, and both her parents, spoke French as well as he did, their diction impeccable.

Eugène now feared a reprieve was not coming, that the foreigners were on their way and could not be turned back, so he began his retreat. He stopped speaking and canceled two lessons. He stayed in his room and perfected his premonition of great trouble on the way: shouting and raised fists, blood, a man moaning. Lucien told him not to be silly, because he would bring on his headaches and that the visitors would only stay a week. But the wires were cut and Eugène refused to be cheered up, and kept sighing deeply. He behaved like a beaten man, and was strangely humble.

The travelers, confident of a warm welcome in Algiers, were waiting to embark at the airport. Because the flight was delayed an hour, Molly and Bertie now had time to take stock of Toby Plunkett and were slightly startled. His appearance, which had made little impact on Molly before, now set him apart, because he seemed to be bulging out of his clothes. A button was missing on his jacket. Although his big, agreeable face seemed scrubbed and his hair clean, he smelled—of mold, Molly thought, or of someone who has been held in a closet, in a cellar, for a long time. Bertie thought the jacket, old as it was, had not been to a dry cleaner. Toby Plunkett, who had never been given a free trip anywhere and was now going to Algiers thanks to an eccentric American whom he had met by chance, was elated by his good luck and talking too much. He carried no luggage, only a huge and torn backpack, very old and so carelessly stuffed that its worn straps barely held in the profusion of lumps. Toby's pockets were stuffed with books. It made him seem even more elephantine, and off balance.

The three of them, waiting for the flight to Paris, where they would spend four hours before Air France delivered them to Algiers, were an odd trio. Toby, on his second chocolate bar, was explaining how much he liked Princeton, which seemed rather English to him, so he jokingly called it Princeton-on-Thames. He was working ten hours a day on his dissertation. "It is on Operation Torch," Toby said. "*The Crucible of Alliance: Strategy, Policy and Combined Operations of the Anglo-American Invasion, North Africa, 1942.* And just like a crucible in a foundry, it was encased in dirt, with bits of dark slag hanging on it." Molly thought words poured from him like yards of cloth in a textile mill. There seemed to be no way to stop the complicated machinery, so she and Bertie went to the ladies' room.

"He told me he can get by on four hours of sleep a night," Molly said.

"How disgusting" was Bertie's comment. She distrusted people who boasted of such abnormal tendencies. On their return, Toby was seen talking to a businessman in his early thirties, explaining how he was on his way to Algiers. The man seemed hypnotized. Toby found him a good listener.

"I first saw Molly Benson in a Princeton bookstore, where I was looking for a copy of a Tintin book—to be precise, *Tintin in Tibet.* I read all the Tintin books as a child. They were a passion of mine, and I haven't outgrown it." The American had once liked Tintin, too, although not at Plunkett's age, which was twenty-seven, so the men were able to go on for fifteen minutes, until the businessman's flight was called. Trotting to the gate, he walked rapidly because he feared Toby might come after him.

As the travelers waited for their flight to Paris to be called, now two hours later for no reason at all, Elliot Stretch, owner of the bookstore in Princeton, was giving thanks. He was relieved to be rid of Molly Benson, who was so self-righteous. It did not count in her favor that she volunteered one day a week to help out because he could not pay a larger staff.

"She is too bossy," he said to his wife, who did the books. "She wants everyone to read Graham Greene and Chekhov and Heinrich Böll or Gordimer, and tells them they should. The other day when she mentioned Graham Greene to a customer, a student mind you, he thought she was talking about the Indian actor with that name. You should have seen Molly's face—she looked whiplashed. She gave him a Penguin edition of *The Honorary Consul* and paid for it herself."

"Well, she did invest seventy thousand dollars in the bookstore," his wife said. "And she means so well. She isn't in the least pretentious or demanding. It's rather sweet that she comes in to work on Thursdays."

"Yes, but she always expects, in that nice way, to be accommodated. If people want to read about animal behavior or how to help their colons, she should let them." That was his last outburst on the subject, and the next two weeks was something of a vacation. It was nice, too, to be rid of Toby Plunkett, who dropped in daily to chat with anyone at all, laughed too loudly, and never bought a book, although he pawed through all the new ones, making comments in his strong voice.

On that day of departure, all the travelers were burdened by books. Being the most practical, Bertie, who knew nothing about any religion, had *Islam for Beginners*, with its charming black-and-white drawings, in pen and ink, and *Understanding Catholicism*, since she had never been in the company of priests and was slightly worried about protocol. Toby had a big paperback, *Modern Algeria: The Origins and Development of a Nation*, among others, and Molly carried *L'Algerie Par Ses Islamistes*, which was in French; a small dictionary, since it was hard to read; and, as a treat, an old copy of *Nineteen Stories*, by Graham Greene, first published in 1947. Toby wanted to skim through it, and said he had read most of the stories, which struck the other two as a silly boast. Bertie always made clear Molly's claim on the author, explaining that they had met when her friend was having lunch years ago at Félix au Port in Antibes when she saw Greene eating there, as he so often did. When he left, Molly realized he had dropped a piece of paper from his wallet when he paid the bill. So she went after him and returned it.

"What was on it?" said Toby, always one for the detail.

"A man's name with a telephone number, not in France. Then I went to his apartment for a drink the next day." It was a telephone number in Managua, but she chose not to reveal this; Greene had been sympathetic to the Sandinistas.

"He must have been lonely," said Toby, tactlessly, as if Molly were the last straw.

Then he began humming the notes of the zither music from Greene's film *The Third Man*, which he had seen three times and, since his mother was always entertained by it, an imitation of Joseph Cotten and Orson Welles, knowing he was a brilliant mimic. His companions were only mildly amused. Molly talked about the scene in the sewer when the American Holley Martins catches up with Harry Lime and hesitates to shoot his old, dear friend despite his crime of selling adulterated penicillin on the black market in postwar Vienna.

"And the little smile Welles gives to tell him to go ahead," she said.

"It wasn't a smile. He gave a tiny nod and closed his eyes," Toby said. "That was the okay."

Molly felt a spike of hatred, knowing he was probably right, and dragged Bertie off to buy magazines, anything, so she would not show her displeasure. Then they all went back to their required books, which were to be of no use to them all in Algeria, but no such suspicion had yet arisen, so they read on and on. Molly even wrote a letter to her husband in Osaka: "We are under way at last, although I am not sure in great harmony. The young Englishman is very competitive and loquacious and he needs to eat all the time. The trip is uncertain, but I have a good deal of money with me—five thousand—to provide security for the Algerians in real danger. Some of it is in my shoes under foot pads, and I don't limp, although it feels peculiar. The arrangement should amuse you. I am happy to hear that Keishiro, the new director, understands your film better than Yoshi and that now everything goes well . . ."

There were several interruptions by Toby, who was on his second gin and tonic, while Molly and Bertie were drinking bottled water, which they believed helped you survive long plane trips. They only ate a few tablespoons of food and some crackers and never crossed their legs during the trip. Like old women, Toby thought.

"I remember an interview with Greene on the *Omnibus* program. A German was asking the questions about his work and the great themes in it. I think Greene told him: 'The hunted man is an obvious one, isn't it?' And then he said something about his characters being at the dangerous edge of things psychologically and sometimes politically." He waited for Molly to be impressed by his prodigious memory, as everyone always was, but she only nodded, because she was remembering *The Human Factor* and how Maurice Castle, an English intelligence agent, was really, for the most honorable reason, spying for the Russians and always felt certain that one day a doom would catch up with him. It did. With the layers of bills inside her shoes, and more inside her underwear, Molly felt a tiny degree of Castle's uneasiness, his ceaseless compulsion to be on guard, and thought that she must behave in a most ordinary and nonchalant way, as Castle had. She feared arrest and interrogation by the Algerian authorities, who would make her take off her shoes.

Once, as Greene wrote of one of his characters, she had the audacity that comes from a complete innocence, but after her brother's death, there was nothing of that left, only a brittle layer of bravery when required.

In New York the passengers who boarded were large, pleasant, and placid, pleased to be going to Paris, where they got off. The new group were all Algerian men—short, very dark, in cheap jackets that did not quite fit. The surprising thing was the amount of stuff they were taking back: boxes tied with cord, old suitcases bursting and locked, shopping bags from Samaritaine or Bazar de L'Hôtel de Ville holding too much. There were toys, appliances, radios, parts of stereos, clothing, boxed cassettes, shoes for men and women all jammed in the bags, which they clutched in their seats. The overhead racks were so jammed that the French stewardess, who did not care for these passengers, spoke sharply to them, but the men did not take offense at her haughty tone, for they were accustomed. Molly and Bertie liked these men, their excitement when the plane lifted, believing them to be the poorly paid Algerians in France who were going home to visit, bearing so many gifts that they could ill afford.

"They're probably going to make money reselling all of it at five times the original price," said Toby, Mr. Know-It-All.

The nightmare began when the flight landed: Nothing in all their travels had prepared Molly and Bertie for such pandemonium in an airport. Toby, accustomed to orderly procedures at Heathrow, knew panic as crowds pushed and shoved. There were three flights now disembarking. One man was even knocked off his feet trying to move his five suitcases. Fierce arguments broke out and were settled; tempers flared and subsided. Lines broke, regrouped, and surged forward, three people abreast. It was Toby who rammed into the mob to claim their bags, and almost lost his balance lifting the luggage.

On the other side of customs, where no one passed the barrier quickly, stood a slight European man, a little smile of welcome and encouragement on his face, beckoning to them to move forward past the men lining up at customs. He said only a few words to a guard, who waved all of them through. Lucien always had a mysterious effect on the surly.

"How kind you are," said Molly, and wondered why he was not wearing a collar and black shirt but an old red sweater and unironed checked shirt. The two women clutched the arms of the good man and would not even let him carry their suitcases in their gratitude. At any rate, they traveled lightly. Lucien led them to an old van, which he had borrowed, since he owned no car, only a bicycle, he explained. That seemed charming to the Americans. Nothing could be seen of the magical city on the dark road, but the air was sweet and seemed to smell of lemon leaves. Lucien drove quickly but not with great skill. He needed new eyeglasses.

At home, he gave them cups of chamomile tea and biscuits that were beige and fluted at the edges from a tin box marked with a French name. In the dimly lit room, with tiny bulbs in the large ornate lamps, they felt comforted and pleasantly sleepy as children might who were winding down.

Molly and Bertie were to share a little suite on the top floor, two beds in one room and a small sitting room. Toby was put up in Eugène's office, where a cot was too small for a man of his heft, but after so many years of meager living as a student he was accustomed to discomfort and almost liked it. It was odd that Eugène was nowhere to be seen. His bedroom, the largest, was at the end of the hall on the second floor, and it was not his way to rise early. Lucien brought him morning coffee. He had not waited up to greet the visitors because of a headache, Lucien explained.

It was actually one of Eugène's small mutinies. He was still wide awake and feeling fine, only peevish that the little group was invading the house when their reasons for the trip were so unclear.

"What do they want here? It's not exactly the most auspicious time for tourists," he had kept saying to Lucien. But Lucien was not a man to probe, to need explanations, to peel apart motives, while his friend was like a ferret and only at peace in bed. Lucien tried to calm him, the old habit.

The next day it was Molly who rose at 6:30 A.M. to open the shutters of the long window in the little sitting room, with its tiled fireplace, long unused, and a dark armoire, its wood splitting from age, that held only three hangers inside. What she saw she was always to love and remember: the wide, sickle-shaped bay of Algiers, the sun making the water so brilliant, the curtain of steep hills, the blinding whiteness of the terraced city rising in the tiers with its pine trees and palms. Molly hung out over the little balcony railing as far as she could, then Bertie did, too, in rapture.

"No wonder the French loved Algeria so much," said Bertie, who was stunned by the view. Between them they had been to France eleven times but never made a trip to any Arab country, yet the old instilled confidence held. It did not occur to them that they were ignorant. When they went downstairs for breakfast, Toby was already eating a baguette and Molly thought, I must give money to Lucien for food. Eugène was, of course, still in bed and Lucien was ready to go to work at the hospital, where he volunteered as an orderly and often worked in the supply room. They saw that the living room was all red, the walls, the couch with red pillows, a chair covered in a large red shawl, and that Lucien wore red socks.

Then the first of many shocks as Lucien gave them coffee that was very strong.

"Father," Bertie was saying, hoping for more coffee as her need was great. He shook his head and corrected her.

"We are not priests. We are members of an order—the Little Brothers of Jesus—founded by Charles de Foucauld," he said. It hurt Molly to hear this, for she wanted him to be a priest so she might learn more about the Church and discuss Graham Greene, but Lucien had not heard of the great writer, which seemed so preposterous that she asked twice.

That night, as they slept, a bomb destroyed the Library of Christian Literature on rue Letelier, below the hideous Cathédral Sacre Coeur. It sold Bibles in ten languages, including Bulgarian and Croat, although stock was often erratic. Five men were killed later that morning walking to their cars in various suburbs, and all over Algiers plans were being made for more assassinations. Lists were precise, attacks were scrupulously plotted, men huddled and were happy with their bloody schemes, and felt surges of hope.

PART TWO

Molly Benson often surrendered to startling impulses, which she preferred to think of as guided dreams. It did not escape the notice of Graham Greene in Antibes after he wrote her that he was rereading *Moby-Dick* in celebration of starting a new book. "I suppose Nantucket is already spoilt and not worth visiting? A summer resort?" It was the only place in North America he wanted to visit. "What has become of it?" he asked.

After receiving an expensive overnight letter, which required his signature, just as he was shaving, he learned that she was making arrangements for him to visit Nantucket— September was a lovely month—where he could stay in a guest cottage owned by her friends. No one would bother him. It was Molly's chance to have him all to herself. "What an impulsive girl you are! You are positively dangerous!" he wrote back. For he had no intention of making the trip and was not pleased by such emphatic invitations. There were so many of them. She was not to know until after his death that his correspondence was immense and that the conscientious man replied to every letter, even when there were far more important things at hand, even a few months before his death. His letters were dictated and sent to his sister in England to type and mail. The dear sister was well supplied with his stationery, and sheets of it had his signature. Letters to Molly were usually short, fitting nicely on one page. After the Nantucket incident, Molly knew she had made a mistake and did not try to lure him to America again.

Algeria was an impulse she chose not to beat down. There was no need to explain it to anyone. Molly thought reverberations from colonial rule were insidious, lasting more than a hundred years after independence whether the inhabitants of a country knew it or not. There were decades of political convulsions. All successful revolutions, however idealistic, probably betray themselves in time, Graham Greene wrote, and this one had. Now a peculiar and still-small upheaval had begun in Algeria, not only against a complacent and fossilized government but against the old masters, who, years after their frantic retreat, had left their footprints, eerie and indelible, almost everywhere. She would have written Greene about the trip, but it was too late. He always understood the persistent pull of the Third World and how, even in discovering what could go wrong, to find some happiness in exploring a region of uncertainty, in guessing where roads went.

It was all very suspect to Arnold Einhorn, Bertie's husband, for in his eyes these places meant dust and boredom and beggars. He saw filthy black cooking pots and vultures, children with skin lesions, and diseased dogs. There was the whispering for bribes. He thought Bertie was swept along in Molly's chaotic tow. Any woman who asked a housekeeper to iron her cotton underpants and fold them a certain way was not cut out to slosh about a desperate terrain.

"Poverty, malnourishment if not famine, AIDS, over-population, unemployment, and appalling hygiene and health care," said Arnold. "How could anyone want to go to those countries?" He was on the telephone to his doctor, also a client, who was reading a recipe for mussels and wanted to know what it meant to take off the "beards."

"Those are the rough hairs on top where the shell opens," said Arnold. "Just pull them off."

The doctor tried to cheer him up. "It's not always hope-less there," he said. "A patient of mine has just come back from Mauritius, which he thinks is getting on its feet."

This did not matter to Arnold. "My wife says she and Molly are uncomfortable in their own country—it's too loud, too brutal, and too much is wrong," he said. The doc-tor clucked as if the language of women were only back-ground music in the elevators of daily life and need not be analyzed. He told Arnold to take the ladies to Montana or Wyoming.

In Algiers, Bertie was fussing, as she always did at the start of a trip, because she was keeping a journal and was unable to conjure a single descriptive detail of a new city. All she could ever manage were the lists of her purchases, the price paid, the atmosphere in the store. At this she was very clever.

That morning the women were waiting for hot water so they could take a shower rather than sit in the discolored old bathtub. It came out in loud snorts through a handheld spray and did not last long. It was curious to be in a house that was indifferent to time and lacked any modern improvement. There was not even a vacuum cleaner, for Lucien swept and mopped the floors and the slate stairs. Here, the technology that had insinuated itself in the poorest cities and impoverished villages across the world was missing. Even the little television set was black-and-white. Eugène asked that they bring a liquid eraser, because he made typing mistakes on his old portable Olivetti typewriter. There was no computer, and neither man had ever touched one. There was not a calculator, a microwave, or a mobile telephone, which would have been practical, although there were few calls. The pilot light on the gas stove frequently went out, and the refrigerator lacked a freezer compartment. Molly found all this rather comforting, since she feared technology and thought it would destroy people's privacy without their noticing it. Every check could be called up on a programmed computer, every telephone call listed, all E-mail messages saved for a sinister reason. There was some small consolation that Graham Greene had not lived to see it flourish so insanely, guarding his privacy as he did. "I am afraid the last few months have been a bit of a nightmare with all the press . . . and photographs. The trouble is one can't even eat in peace and letters are sent to me care of the restaurant Felix and sometimes I am even rung up there on the telephone . . ." he had written her. He had just published a pamphlet, with text in English and French, called *J'Accuse*, on organized crime in Nice, which flourished under the tacit protection of the police and the judiciary. With E-mail and a fax, he would have been a hunted man, the old orderly habits wrecked, the world coming too close.

There was more in the letter. He had broken four ribs just before having to introduce Daniel Ortega at a big meeting in Nicaragua, but he was able to do it with some good painkillers.

"We haven't seen very much of Algiers except our walk along the corniche," said Bertie, looking at her notes. They took their coffee in the living room. Lucien had not yet left for work and was carrying a tray to Eugène. Molly was in charge of their appointments.

"We walked for miles," said Toby, who was blossoming in such abundance of pure light. It had even lessened his indigestion, and he was making an effort to improve his carriage.

"You bought a bracelet in that shop on Didouche Mourad for six hundred dinars," said Molly. "We went to the post office in the place Grand Poste, which is the most beautiful one I've ever seen, all those arches and mosaics and the lovely stamps, and then we walked down rue Larbi Ben M'hidi." It was named for a famous resistance leader who was killed by the French.

"Why do some streets still have French names and others are in Arabic?" Toby said, mouth full. No one knew.

"I've never seen such a beautiful city—the whiteness of it, the cliffs, the harbor, the sea," said Molly. "And now let's get ready to roll." It was her favorite expression under duress, once used by Harry.

Neither woman mentioned to Lucien that his own sister in New York had said he was a priest, because it was easier and she didn't understand what his rank really was. Lucien was always very cheerful in the morning, and it surprised him when others were not. He could not tell with the foreigners, who were gulping down his coffee and seemed full of serious intentions. He had called a taxi driver, who would fetch them in twenty minutes, and said they must be there no later than that. Wait by the police station, Lucien said, and was off to the hospital.

Outside the compound, in the soft, loving sun, they began walking down a narrow street of villas so the driver would instantly see them at the bottom. It was Toby, looking up, who grunted and stopped dead in his tracks. He pointed to the window of a villa where there was a soiled, sheer, white curtain deeply fringed at the bottom. A face peering out, a hand waving. The leering old woman, deformed by heavy makeup and a blond wig, beckoned them to come closer. Years later, in Nice, Toby was to see the same curtain again, remember, and need a strong drink. Molly and Bertie waved back and poked Toby to keep walking.

"She's French and she's a captive there," said Toby, who

wrote little movies in his head. Molly sighed and thought Toby would be their undoing if not watched.

They had just reached the police station at place Allende when a van drew up in front and two handcuffed men were pushed out and shoved like balking animals through the door. One of them wore brown bedroom slippers, and the other was without a shirt, as if they had been taken early in the morning and not given time to dress. Both were bleeding. They were unshaven.

"Dear God," said Molly.

"What shall we do?" said Bertie.

Molly, who passionately felt that all decent people must interfere to save the helpless even if it put them at risk, began hollering and running toward the group. The men turned their heads at the astonishing sight; even the policemen stopped shoving and stood there. What made Molly certain, although she had no experience in these matters, that the prisoners were innocent was their cringing appearance, the disbelief on their faces. She thought guilty men would be prouder and more defiant, carrying themselves differently to the beatings that would come and the long hours of interrogation ahead. She was so fast that she was even able to grab the arm of one of the prisoners, as if to pull him free. One of his bedroom slippers had come off, so he was limping. He was not grateful to Molly, it would be worse for him inside if the police were worked up. The older man, without a shirt, who had been whacked on the head so a trickle of blood was reaching his chin, began to say very softly, "Madame, madame . . ."

She had no idea what to do next, so Molly stood in front of the door of the station, at least five inches taller than anyone else, and for half a minute held everyone up by demanding that she be allowed to complain to the police officer in charge. The two policemen did not understand a word she said and moved to push her aside. It was Ahmed Hocine, the driver hired to take them around, who suddenly appeared, handing out cigarettes, standing in front of Molly and explaining in Arabic that one of the prisoners resembled the husband of a distant cousin whom she was planning to visit so she had mistakenly tried to help him. But her eyesight was very poor. One of the policemen even snickered as Ahmed explained she was just a poor, crazed foreign woman but an important person who knew the American ambassador.

"She sees nothing without very strong American glasses," said Ahmed, who was beginning to enjoy himself. Even the prisoners looked relieved that the matter had been settled, and Ahmed retrieved the lost bedroom slipper and put it back on the foot of the limping man before the group disappeared. He led Molly to the car and rounded up Bertie and Toby, who had been watching from a safe distance.

"Well done, Coral," said Bertie, squeezing the hand of her friend. It was a name from their childhood and sent Molly back into Greeneland, to the Mexico of *The Power and the Glory*. The hunted whiskey priest was helped by an indomitable thirteen-year-old child named Coral. Her father worked for a banana company. When the priest hid in their barn, Coral took chicken legs, tortillas, and beer to the famished man, expecting answers to all her questions. He explained that it was his duty not to be caught, and Coral offered to look out for him if he stayed put. This was impossible. " 'If they kill you I shan't forgive them— ever,' " the little girl said, meaning it. "She was ready to accept any responsibility, even that of vengeance, without a second thought," Greene had written in his novel. Molly was fourteen when she read *The Power and the Glory* and changed her first name to Coral, insisting people call her that. Only Bertie obliged, but it had been more than thirty years since she last used that honored name.

In the backseat, Toby was musing. He did not think congratulations were in order, since Molly had accomplished nothing. It was all very well for her to carry on in this theatrical way, but if a man had tried, he would have been pummeled and found himself injured, on the ground. He said so to Molly, pointing out that she must not take such risks, even though as a woman she could be sure of lenient treatment.

"I wouldn't count on it," Molly said. What a strange woman I am with, Toby thought, and then Ahmed spoke, as if he were addressing high-strung children.

"You are in good hands with me," he said. "But I must ask you to behave correctly." He did not want to frighten them, but he knew they should be warned. He would certainly have to keep an eye on the tall, skinny woman so she did not get all of them in trouble. What a spectacle she put on, he thought.

It was apparent that first day that Ahmed would soon be

their cherished friend, their oxygen, their splendid custodian. He was thirty-eight years old, the oldest of six children, living with his mother, who spoke French more fluently than they did and who loved his car. Bertie thought him handsome. Molly admired his eyelashes and dignified bearing.

"Things are slightly disturbed here," he said. "Not tranquil. You should know this. Two of our own journalists were killed last month, and then some foreigners working for an oil company, very far from Algiers." There was fighting in a section of the Casbah, and a state of emergency was soon to be declared, according to rumors that he, Ahmed Hocine, believed. It would kill business, or maybe not, since people would be afraid to take their own cars, which would identify them to any assassin. It was a very bad business with the Islamistes—the French word for the fundamentalists—but the government, those generals, were no better.

"No better," repeated Molly, echoing Professor Chalk's denunciation. She was wondering why she had never written the essay she planned so many years before, to be titled "Graham Greene's Doomed Children: An Analysis," but it was too hard to begin.

Ahmed drove as if they were being pursued, too fast for the passengers to consult maps to know where they were, so the city and its neighborhoods were to remain a mystery. Molly had handed him a white index card with their destination clearly written, but he hardly looked at it and took them to a suburb with expensive but small houses in the palest colors, little gardens in front, bigger ones in back bursting with bougainvillea. A housekeeper showed them into the living room, where there was a painting by the Algerian artist M'Hamed Issiakhem that the Americans instantly admired. Professor Chalk had sent them here to talk to an old friend, a former government official, whom Chalk said was brilliant and cunning. But Anwar Lejaboul was on the telephone in his office, the door open. The housekeeper was nearly deaf, so it did not matter. They waited in the living room, peering at the painting they coveted. They could hear his voice and strained to understand it but could only pick up patches. Lejaboul was clearly talking to a man in the government, giving advice in the most forceful manner, as though accustomed to obedience.

They could see his ruined, commanding face: An old scar like a ridge lifted the left eyebrow too high and was paler than his skin. It gave him an air of surprise.

"Look, old friend, the government sooner or later must kill all stories of killings by any FIS group, otherwise it will just magnify their power and . . . demoralize people. You know . . . what steps to take. There is always censorship, isn't there?" The men were speaking in French, as if it were easier than Arabic.

Lejaboul, famous for his role in the war of Algerian independence, had quite forgotten who was in his house until Molly produced a letter for him from Professor Chalk, which mentioned the date their little delegation was coming. The Algerian was too well bred to show annoyance. He was writing a history of the struggle for independence and found the telephone his greatest obstacle, and visitors were even worse. All sat down.

"I'm retired now, you know, so I'm out of government," said Lejaboul, but he gave himself away by often referring to "we," as if he still held office or were a trusted adviser. He instantly understood that time spent with this group would be wasted, and sighed. But they were so eager and rapt to hear him out—the thin woman was even taking notes—that he softened and began speaking.

"After independence we envisioned Algeria as leaders of the developing world, the Third World, and the Non-Aligned Movement. The trouble really began with the new constitution when Islamic groups were given the right to form parties of their own, which enabled them to partici-pate in a national election," he said. And the Islamic Salva-tion Front was formed, he told them, leaping over decades, failing to mention that a socialist-style dictatorship, bol-stered by oil and natural-gas deposits, did not dispense the wealth to the people.

"You know it as FIS. By becoming more democratic, we opened the floodgates, but we thought after Saddam Hus-sein's defeat in the Gulf War that FIS was much weaker," he said, smiling at them, as if to gloss over a tiny miscalcula-tion by well-meaning men.

"But the army arrested two prominent leaders of FIS, Abbassi Madani and Ali Belhadj," said Molly, who had done her homework. "And FIS won 188 seats outright, and your party, the FLN, did not even come in second. And then the second round of the legislative elections were canceled!"

"There will be no elections if FIS takes over," said Lejaboul. "And no one wanted an Islamic state coming into existence on the southern rim of the Mediterranean, did they?"

Such a possibility had never occurred to Molly, who suddenly saw an Islamic state in the figure of the Ayatollah Khomeini, that great gargoyle face coming close. In her own country, all Arabs were feared and denigrated. She remembered an ugly little scene at Kennedy Airport in New York: a well-dressed woman shrinking back as though in peril at the sight of an old Palestinian in his Arab headdress and robe as they waited for their flight to Israel. He was surrounded by three hefty sons in T-shirts and jeans, but they could not protect him from the horror on an American face.

The Algerian made a small effort at cordiality and began speaking English, with only a faint French accent.

"Look, when the Islamistes won the first round, the middle class went crazy and said: 'How can you permit this to happen?' When the arrests were made and thousands of FIS followers were sent to detention camps, the middle class went crazy and said: 'Now what will the world think of us?' "

He was not without a mocking charm, so they did not ask why the middle class had to be placated when most Algerians were so poor. Anyway, they knew the answer.

"There was some fighting in the Casbah this morning, we are told. How strange it must be for you to hear this and remember the days when it was your side fighting there against the French," said Molly.

Her comment surprised him, for it meant that she knew something about his country's past, and something about love, which had far more power than politics, and he would not have guessed this looking at her. He made a wry little face and rose to his feet to show, with sufficient politeness, that he must get back to work. Long ago he had felt such love for the Algerians in the Casbah, fighting against those odds, that it had almost affected him like a huge invisible wound.

On a piece of paper he wrote the address of the Algerian Press Association, with a warning: They may not be pleased to see you; some of them are in danger. What he did not tell them was that he was in danger, too, for having written several newspaper articles against FIS. His bodyguard was sitting in the kitchen and slept in the house, in front of the door, on a mat.

"A big man," said clever Ahmed, who knew whom they had seen. "But not so big as before."

Toby began whining that he needed lunch, but the women wanted to push on and see just one more person and then they would have a huge lunch. But right now they must go to rue Abane Ramdane to see the lawyer representing Algerians believed to be FIS. They recognized that the street was named for one of the founders of the old National Liberation Front.

"One of the *neuf historique,* who started the struggle for independence," said Molly.

"Were any of them Islamistes?" Bertie said.

"No."

"So thirty years later any foreign presence, the Christian Western influence, has to be purged," said Toby, as if outlining a thesis in his head.

"Come then, comrades, the European game has finally ended; we must find something different," said Molly, who was quoting the revolutionary psychiatrist and writer Frantz Fanon. His was once a revered name in Algeria, but the young did not care about this, and even Toby did not know who he was until she explained.

Ahmed pointed out the building to them and went back to the car for a nap. The night before, he had quarreled with his younger brother and knocked him down to the floor. Afterward there was no sleep for him, only a white night.

There was one flight up to the lawyer's office, and none of them saw the Algerian man coming down. Midway, he stopped to take out a bent cigarette from his pocket and made as if to steady himself. His face was contorted by distress, but they did not notice. Toby always bounded ahead two steps at a time and was already at the landing. It was Bertie, with her great cloud of frizzled, hennaed hair and her thin silk shirt, who was trying to pass the man. He was lean, with a heavy mustache, like thousands of others in the city. Suddenly, he lost all reason. He went into a rage at the sight and smell of her, as if she were an unspeakable affront. One large, rough hand held her throat and the other hand used his cheap lighter, with its high flame, to burn a chunk of her hair, their faces so close together that they might have been about to kiss. Yelling and babbling, he leapt down the stairs as Bertie began screaming and would not stay still as Molly pressed her own hands against the sparks in Bertie's hair, which was singed in one spot.

So horrified were the two women that they sat down on the stairs, which were filthy; there was a lump of spit on one step. Bertie kept touching her damaged hair to see if she might be bald on that side but did not have the courage to take out a mirror.

"He was obviously insane," said Molly, still not understanding why the Algerian was so outraged by her friend. Toby was at their side, his jaw extended, which meant hard thought, and issued a communiqué. He had a clearer grasp of the problem.

"New precautions are called for. You must both cover your heads with scarves or something, and cover your arms as well." He secretly thought Bertie had a manner of flaunting herself. Since the arms of the women were already covered, they did not reply. Bertie was sent back to the safety of the car in Ahmed's custody. The driver was not pleased to see her in such a state, to hear her gulping and crying. So it was heating up, he thought. All the foreigners would be driven away in a year or two, perhaps sooner, and nothing lay ahead for him but pain and submission. But still he told Bertie that her hair looked fine, no great damage had been done, for he did not want this group to leave the next day in panic.

Bertie, who was always moved to tears by unexpected kindness, began to dribble. She knew she looked frightful, and she believed she could smell her own charred hair. Ahmed said there was no smell.

"You are a wonderful man and your wife is a lucky woman," said Bertie, not guessing that Ahmed's mother had sent his wife back to her family because she did not conceive after five years of marriage. And the wife, who pined for him, was forbidden by her father to see a gynecologist, because the only doctor near them, with a modern office, was male.

"Why does anyone want to make trouble, Ahmed, in this beautiful country?" said Bertie from the back, where she was lying down to compose herself.

"Because our lives are so terrible and our government is run by the military and so little is ever done to help us. You can't blame it on the drop in the price of oil," he told her, thinking of his younger brother, who had probably already signed up with a secret Islamic group. "And FIS speak in plain language. All can understand."

Bertie was almost asleep, her spirit squelched, one hand over the ruined patch of hair. Poor Ahmed, fearing that passersby in the street would see a plump Western woman sprawled in the backseat, was compelled to ask her to sit up and lean against the window. Already, two very young men were peering inside the car at her and making joyful faces at the sight of her knees and small ankles.

The door to the office of Ali Abendour Yacef—a dirty bronze plaque with his name said AVOCAT À LA COUR— was locked, and his voice could be heard on the telephone. Molly knocked twice but still the conversation went on until finally the door was slightly opened and a distinguished man, dressed in a good old gray suit, peered out.

"We are late because a friend with us was attacked on the stairs, her hair set on fire," said Molly, fully aware that once again a man had forgotten his appointment with them and clearly did not want them to enter. She produced her card with the name of the foundation on it—a silly name, the Forward Foundation—which only puzzled him. He did not inquire about the friend set on fire, as if it were an ordinary occurrence.

"The man who annoyed your friend is not himself—he has three sons who have been detained in the desert and he fears they will be tortured or kept there for a long, long time," said Mr. Yacef. He was very wan but well shaven, which Toby thought a good sign, with his necktie loosened so you could see the Pierre Cardin label, and the cuffs of his shirt were only slightly soiled. His desk was covered with dossiers, eight or nine piles of them, held by gray string, so there was barely room to write.

"We have come to impose on you," said Molly, who took the only chair; the other was covered with more files, so Toby was obliged to stand and immediately assumed a military posture.

"To ask your advice on a delicate matter," Molly went on, nervous because the French she had learned in private school was wearing thin. "We wish to buy the safety of a certain writer who has been critical of FIS and wonder if you might arrange a *cessez-le-feu* for him." A cease-fire. She named Tahar Djaout.

"You want to buy an Algerian writer?" the lawyer said, in English, because he could not tolerate the flat stumbling way the American spoke French. He put on his glasses to see if anything in her face revealed a mental disorder, but she seemed perfectly composed and held her hands in her lap. Toby was standing at full attention as if he fancied himself an officer in the Coldstream Guards.

"Why not? We are prepared to donate a thousand dollars in cash this week to help the families of the detained men, but not for weapons, and we need your promise on this. You can be trusted. I have all confidence in you. Take the name of the writer off a death list."

But the lawyer was shaking his head. He had the face of a man who was consulting a compass that was broken. The telephone was again ringing, but he did not want to pick it up in case this peculiar pair really spoke Arabic and were CIA agents. The woman did not seem competent for that, but one could never be sure.

"I would not know who to approach to ask about your writer, and it would be most unsuitable. This is not the time to hope to protect one man. There are many thousands to consider. I am only trying to find out who is detained and where, and appeal for their release." There was a map on the wall, and he made them look at it, pointing out three or four of the detention sites, whose names were too complicated for them to absorb or even write down.

"Here there are nearly four thousand," he said, tapping the map. There was a mournful pause in the room.

"Do you come from the U.S. embassy?" he asked.

"Certainly not," Molly said, sharply. "We have not even been there. It is not my inclination to do so."

"Madame, this is a very strange plan and I have no way of implementing it. There is great bitterness now, and perhaps neither of you are fully aware of what has happened in Algeria." The lawyer spoke English with a heavy French accent, which despite herself Molly found charming. They did not need a briefing, but it came at them.

"Algeria has not been a democracy—we have been ruled by the National Liberation Front since independence, which means the heavy hand of the army. In elections for municipal offices in June 1990—our first multiparty election—FIS won control, and legitimately, of 853 of Algeria's 1,541 municipalities. It received 4.5 million votes, about 54 percent. A huge majority were under thirty."

"It was a vote against the government, not for an Islamic state, is that not true?" said Toby, remembering what a British newspaper had printed. He was getting tired standing up. "A protest vote."

"Yes." So the Englishman is not as dull-witted as he looks, the lawyer thought, and motioned for Toby to take a folding chair in the corner and sit down.

"The president, Chadli Bendjedid, resigned and a five-man Haut Comité d'Etat led by President Mohammed Boudiaf was appointed. The cancellation of the second round of elections for the legislature for January 1992 resulted in great turmoil and clashes. Now—please pay attention—over ten thousand of those detained were held without charges or trial in camps in the desert. In March of this year, FIS was banned. There are many men still detained. Acts of violence have been carried out by security forces. And FIS is not a monolithic group, but made up of several factions not entirely in accord."

Molly slowed down taking notes, which she did very badly. Her handwriting grew huge and she often could not decipher her own abbreviations. It was quite a different story with Harry, whose notebooks were filled with tiny, precise sentences, some even underlined, and she always thought Graham Greene had been just as brilliant a reporter as her brother. She knew this from his articles for magazines, which had been collected by a Canadian professor. In a piece from Paraguay, then in the clamp of a dictator, the writer noted that on the main road to the south, more than half of it unpaved, there were 105 kilometers between two towns. "We had seen twenty-six cars, twenty-four horsemen, and sixteen carts pulled by horse or oxen. The cars had only just won," he wrote. He hated the errors or sloppiness of other journalists and complained when he spotted them, and made notes in the margins of their articles.

The lawyer saw that Molly's thoughts were wandering and cleared his throat and regretted that he was wasting so much time.

"But if the security forces of the government have done great harm, then so have the various factions of FIS, and no one is sure who has done what," said Toby.

"Algerians know the difference," the lawyer said. Molly was leaning over, rummaging in her shoe to pull out a wad of bills. The one-hundred-dollar bills were in the right shoe and in her sock.

"Please take this for the families," she said. For only a moment the lawyer imagined returning it, but then changed his mind, for it was urgently needed. That night, he told his wife that the money was slightly damp and that the benefactor, an American, was *"un peu dingue"* or pretty crazy. But in the office as he took the contribution he gave her a small gift, a warning.

"It is not the best time for you to see our lovely country," Mr. Yacef told them. "There is a deep feeling against foreigners. It is believed by many that France has kept the government propped up for many years, and the United States has gone along. Foreigners remind us of our unhappy past."

"But surely you were educated in France," said Molly, which was unwise, for it offended him although it was perfectly true, and she took her leave, with Toby at her heels.

"Really, Molly, I think it's disgusting that you give money to FIS," Toby said.

"I didn't. I gave money to women and children."

"If that's what you choose to believe," said Toby, deciding to be a gentleman and not quarrel. Americans think they can buy everything, Toby thought, but I suppose it's worse in other places, like Saudi Arabia and Kuwait. It suddenly struck him that they were on a futile trip. It would take months to sort things out, and the pretense that they were helping writers in danger was wearing him down. He wanted to be at home with his books.

Molly did not plan to explain anything about Bertie's hair to Lucien when they returned home, for the two men never spoke of turmoil in the city. But Lucien, home early from the hospital, was in the red living room, talking with an Algerian man in hushed voices.

"We can keep him here when our guests go, but they plan to stay a few more days. Tell your wife this. Stay calm, dear Ali. How old is your child?" The other man mumbled that his boy was now seven. Then he broke off, hearing the three of them come up the stairs. Bertie, who had the best hearing, took in some of the conversation. Then Molly called out to Lucien that they were going to their rooms and Toby was coming with them to wash up, and heard the men go on talking. In their little suite they looked at each other, astonished. They sat on the two beds in a huddle.

"He is going to hide a family in the house," Bertie said. "The trouble is there is a child who will make noise and will want to play outside, I think."

Molly was ashamed of herself for thinking that Lucien had perched himself far above the vicious fray and noticed nothing. She had been harsh about his keeping such a distance. He and Eugène, with their fixed little habits and different kinds of fussiness, impressed her as men in a quarantine ward by their own choice. Once, in speaking of Harry Benson, Bertie told Lucien that Molly's murdered brother had covered many wars, starting with Vietnam.

"And is that over now?" asked Eugène.

"Yes, it ended in 1975, seventeen years ago," Bertie said. "And the Americans lost."

In their bedroom, they decided they must not spend an extra day in the house when a family was in peril and needed their rooms. They would simply say there was nothing more to do and go to the airport.

"What is hurtful is that Lucien has said nothing to us about the new guests, as if we were not to be trusted," said Bertie, rubbing more vitamin E cream from a tube onto her burned hair.

"You have to earn trust," said Molly. "We've just been a nuisance to them. And we've been secretive with him as well."

Then they heard Lucien calling up to them that there was a lovely couscous for dinner, which he was warming. The wife of one of the other orderlies in the hospital had sent him leftovers, and she was famous for her couscous. It had only to be very slowly heated. Toby groaned with pleasure. He did not guess that it was a rather coarse dish made of semolina and lamb with vegetables and beans, which upset his English digestive tract. At the dinner, a pretense was made that it was delicious. They ate sitting around the coffee table, plates in their laps.

Conversations at dinner were often splotchy, so it was clever of Bertie to mention the painting they had seen by M'Hamed Issiakhem, for Lucien leapt to his feet in excitement. He went to the fireplace and returned with a copy of Issiakhem's famous painting—it was a postcard, really, not more than three by five inches—called *The Suffering Christ*. It was in strong strokes of red and purple and black, the long thin face slashed, the mouth open, the eyes almost closed. It made them shudder, but it was beautiful, too.

"It was a gift from a patient," Lucien said. "To think a

Muslim could paint our Lord on the cross with such feeling." He also showed them a present from a patient whom he had helped nurse: a cross made of plastic tubing and bound by surgical thread. Molly thought it repulsive.

He wanted the visitors to understand the lovely generosity he found in so many Algerians, which always delighted and moved him. It startled Lucien to realize how happy he had been in Algiers, as if now, as the murderous commotion began, the peacefulness would disappear. Perhaps he had not earned the right to be so happy.

The guests offered to wash up, were refused, and went to bed early. Lucien thought they looked a bit glum, although he saw nothing unusual about Bertie's hair.

"Perhaps we should plan an excursion for them," he said to Eugène when they were alone. "I might take them to the Casbah to see Father André in his school."

"To the Casbah?" said Eugène, putting away the dishes. He thought that very unwise.

Later that night, Toby crept out of bed to have a private talk with Lucien, who slept on the couch in his underwear, arms crossed over his chest, looking like an embalmed saint. But he woke immediately and saw that Toby had an urgent matter to discuss. It was the loathsome blond Frenchwoman, grinning and beckoning to him as she drew back the soiled fringed curtain and leaned out the window so he might better see her. He went weak with terror, which he could not explain. She was like a vile lizard wanting to lick him. He sat in the red living room, which he found suffocating and cheerless, trying to describe how disgusting she was. The kitchen faucet dripped.

"Oh yes, we know she is there. She has been in that house for thirty years and does no harm. She never goes out."

"Is she a prisoner?" asked Toby, in his rushed way. "Why didn't she leave in 1962 with all the others?" He meant the French colonialists.

"She wanted to stay in Algeria and knew she would be protected. She is taken care of by a very old Arab man who once loved her."

"Loved her? Was that permitted?" The idea sent Toby reeling.

"I suppose some people were offended. She was a prostitute, a rather famous one," said Lucien, who sensed that Toby was not a worldly young man, for his cheeks were now blotchy.

"How many left?"

"There was a great exodus—1,380,000 got out, mostly to go to France. They had to go very quickly and leave everything behind. People were allowed two suitcases, and fought to get on ships. We came two years later."

"The suitcase or the coffin," said Toby, who had read that. He felt calmer talking to Lucien, and was almost certain now that the ghastly woman could not ensnare him.

But still Toby did not leave, so Lucien listened. Everything in the last forty years had taught him how to do this. He could recognize a man in pain, although he could not easily detect its source. Toby was suffering one of his spasms of shame, knowing he was being cruel to the poor Frenchwoman. His mind was on hell.

"It's not a place, is it? We carry it around with us, a hell that separates us from all that is kind and good and generous," Toby said. Lucien, who did not quite follow, told him not to worry and to go to bed. As a consolation, he gave Toby two biscuits from the tin box.

Since Ahmed had gone to deliver a note to the address of the writer Tahar Djaout, there was a free day as they waited for a reply. Molly pretended to be pleased to go to the hospital with Lucien. Toby wanted to go to museums and to the British embassy for any briefing they might provide. Bertie wanted to sit in the sun, hoping that if she could appear tanned, her bald spot might be less shocking. It had been her deepest wish, before the attack on her, to photograph the place des Martyrs and boulevard Che Guevara, but she was not up to it anymore. Toby claimed the car and the driver, because his plans were the most complicated. His energy had become irritating to the women.

Molly went with Lucien by foot to the old French hospital, and he clearly liked the fifteen-minute walk, downhill all the way. It was his day to work in the supply room and to keep inventory of the medications and antibiotics. It was a large building, now a faded yellow, with a long veranda in the front. There were a few yellow flower beds on the grounds in need of watering, and some people were sitting on the grass under a tree. They walked to the third floor, down several long halls, to the supply room. The patients' wards seemed crowded but no more so than in a New York public hospital, Molly thought. The rooms were airless, because the shutters were nearly closed to keep the rooms dim, but there were ceiling fans that still worked.

Patients lay in compliant discomfort. You heard the occasional moan or the cry for a nurse, since there were no buzzers. The floors were clean but needed waxing. A few doctors were making rounds but not in the brisk, self-important way of American physicians, who did not have time to sit by the sick.

Molly knew enough about poor countries to expect nothing more of the hospital, but in the eyes of Lucien it was a marvelous place, where the sick were always healed and their bodies restored. The climate of course helped, too, he said, remembering the cold of Brittany and a childhood spent shivering.

In the supply room, with its empty shelves, male orderlies and others whose jobs were unclear to her came in with scraps of paper to show Lucien what the doctors or nurses needed and did not seem surprised, or upset, when he looked and found there was nothing. He would smile at them, shaking his head a little, as if deeply sorry for the shortages. The hope of the Third World, Molly remembered—that is what Algeria had once been called.

People who came in with requests liked to chat with Lucien for a few minutes. Since Molly had the one chair, they sat on a crate by his desk. A man in his late fifties, an X-ray technician, who wanted nothing, dropped by to tell Lucien about the trouble in his neighborhood in Bab-el-Oued the week before. There had been gunfire, and the police had searched two houses and dragged two men to the street, where they were shot at point-blank range. Everyone on the street knew the victims were only vendors. Since he himself was a deep sleeper, he only had a glimpse of the corpses before an ambulance came, but you could hear women shrieking from their open windows and his own wife, who had always bought fruit from one victim and fish from the second dead man, began to have a nosebleed from the terror of it. She was quite a bleeder, that one.

"I set up night ambushes and the other fellows were killed. They got me," the X-ray technician said, of the old war. "But I forgive the French. I suffered; everyone did. I still have the scars of cigarette burns on my leg from an interrogation, and—" He broke off out of courtesy, thinking Molly might be too sheltered to hear the ghastly details. There were two scars on his face as well, which looked like deep punctures of some kind. She knew more than he dreamed: torture in Vietnam and in Cambodia, torture in Chile, torture in East Timor, torture in El Salvador, torture in Gaza, torture everywhere.

"We were fighting for our independence, and the Islamistes want to destroy it. The French weren't my Muslim brothers, and I forgive them. But now we are being betrayed by our own," the X-ray technician said. He was eating part of Lucien's sandwich as lunch but refused some fruit. No time. An X-ray machine was broken and the patients were piling up.

"A very good man," said Lucien, looking around the empty shelves. Most of the medicine came from France, but there was not enough money to order more. He lifted his clipboard and began the depressing inventory. Molly said she must go home to keep Bertie company, for she was in a morose state. Lucien, counting the boxes of penicillin, nodded.

"The worst may yet come, but we must stand strong. Eugène and I have talked about it and decided not to leave. I think God would want us here." He blushed slightly saying this, feeling presumptuous, and she embraced him lightly for the first time.

Hoping to find the women's bathroom, Molly took a wrong turn on a floor for female patients, where there was more noise, a high-pitched chattering among the women, who were happy to discuss their surgeries, their fevers, their doctors, and their children. She did not see that a slight man in a wrinkled blue uniform was washing the floor and leaving large puddles as he did so, as if wringing the mop once in a while were too arduous or complex a procedure. She slid and fell.

He stopped mopping and leaned over her but did not offer his hand. He had the crumpled face of a man in deep distress, and his eyes kept shifting as if an enemy might approach. Molly asked him to give her a hand; her skirt was sopping wet in back.

"But I am Ben Bella," the man said. She clumsily rose on her own and faced him. Of course he was not Ben Bella, once a hero of the National Liberation Front and the first president of independent Algeria, who had been ousted and imprisoned for many years.

"I have been in prison too long and badly treated," the man said. "You know that, don't you? I was betrayed."

"Yes," said Molly, who suddenly remembered that Ahmed told her that Ben Bella had once wanted all government employees to wear Mao jackets, which she thought was not a bad idea. To her great relief she saw a doctor in a perfectly laundered white coat approach, tiptoeing around the little lakes of soapy water, and called to him.

"Don't be afraid," the doctor said. "He is quite harmless. He is one of the patients from the Centre Psychiatrique des Anciens Combattants who do odd jobs in the hospital, because we are so shorthanded. He will go home in a special bus. He thinks he is Ben Bella? Maybe Ben Bella was a hero to him. Many of those patients are delusional, you know."

The doctor spoke softly to the man, a hand on his shoulder, and the deranged fellow began to wring out the mop on the appliance on top of his bucket. He liked easy instructions.

The doctor walked with Molly to the nearest exit, and when she asked him the time, since she did not own a watch, he said it was 3:15 P.M. on April 30. They shook hands, and he said it was too bad about her skirt, which was dripping. She loved April 30. It was momentous; it still enclosed her in some sort of happiness. It was the day, long ago, that the Vietnam War came to an immense, and startling, halt and, years later, the day that Graham Greene took her to watch a dance outdoors in Antibes. He was not what she expected to find, having always pictured a frail man of weary demeanor. He was very tall and quite graceful, with wide shoulders, someone who had not thickened with age or been dimmed by it. The face, once beautiful, was now interesting, with nice large ears, a boyish mischievous smile, and blue eyes that watered slightly and saw everything. He was not pompous; he was not condescending. Instead of the spent and melancholy genius she imagined, he was a man easily amused. Once or twice, they both laughed. In her wet skirt, which was making small puddles as she went, she wished the day might last longer, and walked back to the house in slow steps, remembering Antibes.

In his office, Eugène was giving a lesson to seventeen-year-old Dalila, who was complaining bitterly, during a conversational exercise in French, that her class had made a school trip to the Grand Monument aux Martyrs, her third compulsory visit. Because of the huge stylized palm fronds with an eternal flame in the center, Dalila said it looked like *"une banane renversé."* A banana turned over. Eugène looked sternly at her and said a million Algerians had died in the war and a well brought up young woman would be respectful of that. There would be no more conversation if she was going to be impudent. Dalila faked remorse.

"Ah, attention, ma petite. Nous devons faire la conjugaison des verbes intransitifs qui prennant l'auxiliaire être," he went

on. It was easy enough for Dalila, who rattled away, pleased with herself.

One of Eugène's most mutinous pupils, a sixteen-year-old named Zohra, came an hour after Dalila flounced out. She was assigned to write a short essay on the religious philosophy of the French scientist Pascal and knew Eugène, with his round, ratlike face, would gnaw at each line. "Remember what Pascal said, that a man who starts looking for God has already found him," Eugène called out to her, almost in falsetto, as she was leaving. Only the arrival of the foreigners kept her coming back, for she felt half dead from boredom and last week had decided not to go on with her lessons with Eugène. It was delightful to see Toby outside, slumped in the old orange deck chair, reading his book on modern Algeria. The chair was tilting under his immense weight; one huge leg crossed to prop up the book. She began circling him, but Toby was unaware that she was flirting, oblivious as to how she was using her mouth and her hips. He only stared at her with shy and wary eyes, for he was always awkward with young women. Even his girl-friend in England, Fiona, teased him about it. "Molly and Bertie are out," he said, hoping she was looking for them. What she saw as indifference infuriated Zohra, so she took away his book, placed it on the ground, and sat on his lap. This behavior was impossible with Algerian men, or boys, but she hoped Toby might be good practice for some romantic encounter abroad. His jaw dropped in shock, for no female had ever behaved so brazenly, and he wondered what Fiona would tell him to do. Then Toby simply heaved himself upright, making Zohra slide off him, and stalked to his room with his book, leaving her dumped on the grass.

The spiteful child took her revenge soon enough. Two days later, she went back in the house when everyone was out and Eugène was taking his daily afternoon nap—his hearing was not acute in any case—and tiptoed to the rooms of Molly and Bertie. She only wanted to see their things. It was Bertie's expensive lace-trimmed underwear and a white cotton nightgown with a shirred waist that pleased her the most. Nothing Molly owned was of interest, all of it looked so old and plain. She tried on Bertie's tortoiseshell bangles and silver pendant, sprayed her wrists with her eau de toilette, arranged one of her long silk scarves in a turban, and used Bertie's rouge to brush on long, dark red slashes on her cheekbones. The fear of discovery made it all the more fun. Zohra rummaged, she cavorted, she posed before the mirror.

That same afternoon, Molly and Bertie went to have their hair washed as the water pressure in the house was too fickle for a decent shampoo. They were looking for a beauty salon in the discouraging, vast lobby of the El Djazair Hotel, where the furniture was so inconveniently arranged. The oversized purple couches needed a happier color and were the reason that the lobby looked so mournful.

A tall man approached, taking off his dark glasses, his face quite puffy. He bowed slightly to Molly as he shook her hand. His name meant nothing; it sounded like Peter Way-wup of Reuter's.

"I was a pal of your brother's," he said. "Well, so many of us were. He is greatly missed. I was shocked to hear what happened at the checkpoint. A nasty business."

"He wasn't killed at a checkpoint," said Molly.

"Of course," the man said, realizing his mistake in mentioning it, for she had probably been provided with another version.

"Where did you know Harry?" asked Bertie.

"We were together in Peshawar during Afghanistan," the Reuters man said, looking for a business card in his wallet but discovering he had run out. He saw that the women found this odd and looked sideways at each other.

Asked what they were doing in Algiers—"of all places," the man said—the two women sang out, almost in unison, that they were only passing through and would be gone the next day.

"I'm glad to hear it," he said. "Things are going to get messy." The women sat down on one of the purple couches, which were so huge that four more people could have been seated. Molly was hardened to such encounters. She still remembered the visit of one of Harry's oldest friends, who had come to see her in Princeton a few years ago clearly expecting a drink. There was nothing but ginger ale and no ice, for she had forgotten to put water in the trays. The restless man went to the bookshelves and pulled out a novel with the Karsh photograph on the back cover. "Ah, the elusive Graham Greene," he said. She did not like this photograph. His right hand was raised to his chin, with the index finger lifted to conceal the upper lip.

"He wasn't elusive," Molly said. "He wrote about smoking opium in Indochina and taking Benzedrine once while he wrote two novels at the same time and its awful effect on his marriage. He has referred to his infidelities. He never concealed his politics or his friendships. There are three books of autobiography—not the usual tendencies of the elusive man."

"Didn't Harry prefer John le Carré?" the friend asked, and the meeting ended on this sour note.

They hoped to be diverted by watching people in the hotel lobby, but only one woman, with lacquered platinum hair and the ankles of a horse, strolled by them.

"That man was certainly suspect," said Bertie.

"A spook. Correspondents don't usually wear cuff links, do they?" said Molly. "And then Harry wasn't in Peshawar. He was dead by the time the Americans were writing about the war in Afghanistan. And why did he think Harry was killed at a checkpoint?" She hated that part.

The two of them, who felt a profound suspicion of their own government, knew that Molly was not important enough to warrant ongoing high-level surveillance, but both women believed certain of her donations singled her out for trouble. Among the trespasses there was money for medicines in Cuba, money for the Sandinista tuberculosis clinics in Nicaragua, money for the rebel hospitals in El Salvador, money for Palestinians in Gaza, and so forth. Surely these had not gone unnoticed in some agency in Washington, D.C., that kept an eye on errant citizens. The two women were not to blame: What kept on blooming inside them came from the old root planted so many years ago by Americans opposed to the Vietnam War and a president who wanted to punish all of them.

They decided to skip the shampoos and go home. It was instantly apparent that someone had been searching their rooms. Bertie's nightgown was folded in a careless way. The bedroom smelled of her eau de toilette, and her rouge was left out on the sink. Molly added her own complaints, but calmly.

"What shall we do?" said Bertie.

"Nothing. Don't even mention it to Lucien. I have all the money with me, so that's okay, and we'll go on as usual. I wish we had locks for our suitcases, but maybe the police are not coming back. It's obvious we aren't dangerous, isn't it? How I wish we hadn't bumped into that man at the hotel."

She knew now that her own version of Harry's death could not hold up forever, however tightly she held on to it. Some time ago it had been suggested by a freelance photographer in Salvador that Harry had died of a heart attack and his careening car had alarmed some soldiers who opened fire. Another woman photographer had told Bertie that Harry had spoken of a headache that morning at breakfast, took medicine, and perhaps did not see the soldier who waved at him to stop. Molly did not want to think of Harry dying in such a haphazard and ridiculous way. She almost preferred that he had been targeted for death by an underpaid and bored officer who held a list of foreign trouble-makers in the large press corps and was told he must take action. So the captain did.

Molly began to crave sleep as she sometimes did when a day began to shrivel fast, and a slight lower back pain made itself known. Despite bouts of ferocious energy, she loved to sleep. No bed was too lumpy or too small for her, even the one at the small hotel in Antibes where she had stayed. There, the mattress in her small room had felt like spongy loaves of damp bread, but it hardly mattered. Extreme happiness made her want to sleep, as did sorrow. "It's your thyroid," her mother said. "Have it tested." Now she settled down for a nap in a meager bed that creaked and whose white sheets were mended in thick little scars. Bertie went searching for a bucket so they might wash their own hair—it was more important to her than to Molly. She always hoped to dream, even during short naps, but it rarely happened, so that waking up there was nothing to remember, only a slight sludge to clear away. Harry did not come back to her, and Graham Greene, in the grave for nearly a year, would not visit. She tried to compel him by conjuring his face just before she went off, or talking to him. Still, he did not humor her. His own dreams—warnings, premonitions, vignettes, material for a new book—seemed a marvel. In one dream he helped capture Hitler, in another he was the English poet of the Great War, Wilfred Owen. There were never nightmares. He told Molly how he kept a record of them for twenty-five years. Dying, at the L'Hôpital de la

Providence in Vevey, he asked the woman he had loved for so long to see to the publication of a dream diary. "As a kind of farewell, Graham opens a door for us on the world of his own," Yvonne Cloetta wrote in a foreword to the little book. That was his last title, *A World of My Own*.

t was Molly's intention to talk to Ahmed about buying cheap small locks for their baggage, but she forgot soon enough when she saw the inside of his car the next morning.

There was blood everywhere, in huge smears, which he had hoped to remove with water and a strong brush, having worked at it for more than an hour. But the poor man used very hot water and soap instead of cold water and salt, for he did not know about these things and was not about to consult his overwrought mother.

"There was an accident, and I took one of the victims to the hospital," Ahmed said, not looking Molly in the face. The backseat was still wet, because earlier that morning he had tried again to scrub the blood out, but the stains, although paler, persisted. The two women didn't want to take their places in the car, so Molly ran back to the house to fetch towels and two of her old cardigans, which she laid down on the damp seats. The driver looked agitated. He feared the car was ruined.

"Ahmed, I hope everything is all right," said Molly. "We will buy some peroxide." He needed to talk but said nothing, a lifelong habit, and she guessed this. Coming from a country where people were encouraged to tell everything about themselves—in the mistaken belief that it would be of great benefit—Molly admired him for his silence.

The night before, the wife of an old friend had telephoned, begging Ahmed to come right away. Between her spasms of sobbing and hoarse breaths, she explained that her husband was bleeding on their bed and that she could not lift him herself. She could not even drive the car to the hospital.

"He went outside for a stroll and to smoke a cigarette," the woman said. "He was shot." It happened only two blocks away, and since he was able to tell them where he lived, two passersby had half carried him home to her and lain him down.

By now, even the mattress was soaked. Ahmed tore up a sheet and wrapped strips tightly around the thigh but did not know what a ruptured femoral artery will do, so the blood came rushing through those thin tight barriers. He carried his friend to the backseat of his car, talking all the way, as if to forestall a catastrophe. He did not understand that it was already too late. Ahmed delivered a dead man to the hospital.

Dread now covered him like a shroud. He thought that what a man needed in such times was good luck, and he had never been blessed that way. Maybe these foreigners will bring me luck, Ahmed thought. But he knew better: There was something sad in Molly's long, narrow face, and lucky people did not look sad.

"Do you need money, Ahmed?" asked Molly softly. Toby was off on his own, taking taxis.

"Yes," he said. "It is to help a family." From the pocket of her skirt she handed him a wad of dinars, held together by a rubber band, which she did not count. On one side of the bills was an antelope with mountains in the distance. There was a moral simplicity about this small act that her grander schemes always lost.

Ahead was a long, dull day, with two fruitless interviews with men that Professor Chalk had urged them to see, since they were linked with FIS. But they had nothing to say and looked uncomfortable, as if this female presence were presumptuous beyond belief, so Molly's voice dried in her throat. Bertie looked frightened and kept her head down.

"Surely you want your side of the struggle to be known," Molly said. But they did not and would not speak to her directly, using a teenage boy in jeans to translate.

"No, there is no need," said the first man. "Especially in your country." His eyes were slightly yellow, and as he spoke he stared at the green linoleum floor as if to deny her existence.

"We mean no harm," said Molly, but the teenage boy seemed uncertain of the meaning of this, since he had had only four years of French in school before all instruction in this language was stopped.

It turned out to be a radiant and busy day for Toby, and

he was puffed up with pleasure at all that he had achieved—and did not notice, or perhaps care, that the two women looked listless and worried. He ordered them to assemble in their suite to hear him out. "Yes, sahib," said Bertie. That morning, by chance, he had gone to the El Djazair Hotel to a little kiosk by the driveway to poke around. Once called the St. Georges, the hotel had been Allied headquarters in 1942 and General Dwight Eisenhower and Winston Churchill strolled together in the gardens to plan for a world of Anglo-Saxon dominance. In the kiosk, which sold old postcards, he hoped a picture of the two leaders could be found.

The old man in attendance was pleased to see Toby, for his morning had been dreadful. He had been threatened and insulted by the cousin of one of the waiters in the restaurant. All foreign magazines, especially from France, were not to be sold.

"No more of this French filth," said the cousin. "We consider it sinful." The old man did not argue that the overseas edition of *Le Monde* was only words, no pictures, but wishing to be seen as obedient, grabbed the offending papers and magazines in his own hands and shouted: "Out, out, all of it." *Marie Claire, Paris Match,* and an old issue of French *Vogue* were now carriers of a disease.

When the fat foreigner came in, with his odd bulging blue eyes, it gave him pleasure, for business was very bad. He handed Toby a shoe box of old postcards and let him slowly rummage. Toby peered at each one, front and back. To his astonishment he found two postcards with portraits of Charles Eugène de Foucauld, who inspired the founding of the Little Brothers of Jesus in 1935. How pleased Lucien and Eugène will be, Toby thought, and also bought some postcards of the old French garrison at Blida and French troops on parade. He gave the old man too many dinars in his happiness over the portraits of Foucauld.

But that was not what he wanted Molly and Bertie to hear. At the British embassy, he had stumbled upon a most engaging fellow, who was happy to talk, on yet another uncertain day.

It was clear that he felt the women were denied such privileged access and that his citizenship required a decent accounting of the danger for them all. Britons did not fail one another abroad.

"All nonessential foreigners are advised to leave at once. We already know about the elections at the end of December 1991 in which FIS won a stunning majority and the president then resigned. The second round of elections, to be held January 16, 1992, were canceled and there were widespread demonstrations by FIS."

"We already know all this," said Bertie, but Toby was rolling on. "Over ten thousand Algerians held without charges or trial in internment camps but many have been released. FIS is banned. Human rights abuses and violations have been committed by the security forces and armed groups. Families of security forces and many civilians risk being killed. There seem to be many armed and militant Islamic groups—at least six—but their initials are too confusing to get straight.

"Since last year, Algerian security forces have increasingly resorted to torture of detainees in their custody, and the method of torture most commonly used—"

"Oh, stop," said Molly.

Toby went on, skipping over details of torture. "Very well. You should know that the poor civilians are in a terrible bind. Even teachers are threatened by the extremists."

He was standing in front of the fireplace, whose tiles had a blue and brown design that Molly loved. She and Bertie were sitting on forlorn straight-back chairs, whose seats could barely support their weight. Molly asked about Ben Bella, remembering the man with the mop.

"I think he felt a socialist nation to be totally consistent with an Arab-Islamic heritage, especially if Islam could be understood in its true progressive sense," said Toby. "But there were many who felt that this was a road laid out by foreigners and totally alien to the Algerian cultural heritage. Francophony meant secularization, and Arabization was inherently tied to Islamization." He had read all this in books, but pretended otherwise to impress the women.

Since Lucien had asked them not to go out at night, even if they were longing to have dinner in a restaurant, they trooped downstairs when he called. A great fuss was made when the postcards were presented, and Lucien put his on the fireplace by the cross and the painting of Jesus. It was Eugène who made the mistake, in his pleasure at the little gift, of asking Toby about his historical research, and he began with the Allied invasion of North Africa, which was not of interest to anyone in the room.

"At first, the Americans and British could not agree on strategy—of course Montgomery had his offensive in Libya and Egypt against Rommel's forces and the U.S. were having setbacks in the Pacific. But they finally succeeded in getting the resources after dealing with Admiral Jean-Louis Darlan, who was the Vichy governor of French territories. He had the good sense to see that he had best cooperate with the Allies. They needed the air base for bombing raids, and to hit German subs and cut down German forces. Half a million Germans surrendered in Tunisia, and many historians have not paid sufficient attention to this campaign."

"Oh my," said Molly, thinking of the young corpses in the African sun and sand.

"Who was Montgomery?" asked Bertie, and earned Toby's deepest scowl. He found so many Americans uneducated.

It was up to Molly to lead them out of the North African campaign, and the desperate struggle, by asking about Foucauld, who had loved his years of solitude in the desert and the self-sacrifice it demanded.

"He sought to bring Christianity to the Muslim desert, not by preaching but by doing good," Lucien said.

"As you do," Molly said, thinking of the Algerian who was depending on him for sanctuary.

But Eugène needed to be heard; there were so few chances for him to be interesting.

"We all had to spend a month in the desert before being admitted to the order," Eugène said, winding up very fast. "Each man had almost nothing—a blanket, some water, a little food. The solitude was the test, not hunger or the cold at night. It was hard for a man of my sensibilities. I grew up in a very poor family, so the hunger was familiar. You begin to hallucinate halfway through it. I thought I was a guest at a feast, helping myself to huge portions of lamb, which turned out to be tiny insects in my little bowl, and I heard myself howling. Ah, honestly, if you can get through that, you can get through anything."

Lucien looked mildly disapproving but did not interrupt as Eugène went on about the damage done to his nervous system. He too had been through the same ordeal, but thought it highly self-indulgent to refer to the hardship when it was a privilege to honor Foucauld, the hermit, the scholar, the saintly man.

"Once I thought I saw seagulls," said Eugène, "above all that sand."

That very night, Ahmed was having another row with his seventeen-year-old brother, Saadi, who, although much slighter, was not cowed. Saadi was going out late at nights and unwilling to explain his whereabouts. In fact, he did not even bother to lie. Ahmed cornered him.

"You will get into trouble," he said, beginning the quarrel. "The police will pick you up." Saadi, who was unshaven and tired-looking, had the air of a fugitive. He only came home to eat and to sleep. He carried a long knife, which now rested on a table near his cassette player. They were in his bedroom so that their mother could not hear, for she was excessively protective of Saadi, her last child, who was jaundiced at birth.

"Let them. Thousands of us are already in prison. What we are doing is larger than my life. I am only a little worm. Only you, Ahmed, cannot see beyond your precious car. Algeria is sick, diseased by our leaders, and the lingering poison of the French, whom we imitate in all things. So we are not an Arab nation at all, and the faithless pull us down to disgrace. We must begin the great purge. Islam will cleanse and restore us."

Ahmed was astonished, since there was something co-herent in what the boy said, and a brightness in his thin, wolfish face, which was usually sulky and secretive. He did not know how to argue, how to plead, or how to reason. He did not care about the despicable generals who ran things or that 95 percent of the Algerian population still spoke French, for Saadi was now ranting about this, and much else. Ahmed waited for him to quiet down. But he was the one who began shouting.

"Oh lunatic, oh jackass," he said. "How can you believe in such shit and put all of us in danger if you join with FIS or any of their armed thugs? They are madmen. Now, you stay in your room for twenty-four hours and see what a fancy prison might be like." He slammed the door shut and wedged a chair under the knob so that it could not be turned. Then, as an extra precaution, he hammered a nail in the wall and strung some heavy cord from it to the door-knob so that nothing would permit the boy to escape.

"Now you will find the right path," Ahmed hollered at

the prisoner, and turned to face his mother, who was aghast, ready to begin weeping as she often did, believing that it would make her sons ashamed of their violent quarrels. But the tears had no effect on them. They assumed that all women wept when men went at each other.

"He wants Algeria to be an Islamic state, he is for FIS," Ahmed said. "I think he has joined them."

"Well, why not? How could it be worse for us? The roof needs fixing, and the rain comes in. There are broken panes of glass. The stove is forty, fifty years old. You can barely buy gasoline for the car. Food prices are dreadful, we have no clothes, the buses don't come or they break down so I rarely see your sisters and their children . . ."

She had sung out the same complaints before in her high, nasal voice—Arabic was a fine language for anguish—so he turned away and thought once again that he was incarcerated by his own family. No one need bother to send him to jail. He was held in this house by his belief in love and duty, but they inflicted a humiliation of a kind he could hardly describe. He had quite forgotten, since his wife was sent away, what it meant to feel happiness of any kind.

In the sparse bedroom, Molly was admiring two large cobwebs in the corners of the very high ceiling that looked lacy in the morning light. Bertie was dawdling in the bathroom when Molly called to her; there was a crankiness in the air, which she hoped to dispel.

"Today we must see Tahar Djaout," said Molly. It was a Thursday, and she was waiting for Bertie to stop looking at herself in the mirror.

"No, I think we should book our flight home," said Bertie. "Now."

Molly was shocked, for she was unaccustomed to Bertie in a mutinous mood. But they had run only half the course and must not give up until they had helped the gifted Algerian writer. Surely this is what Graham Greene would have wanted her to do. The day was beginning to flatten her and she began deep breathing, as if this might divert the sadness she felt. It came, as always, from the fear that she was wasting her life, hiding behind a hill of money and dispensing it as easily as a passerby might drop coins in the paper cup held out by a homeless man. And the trips were clearly an escape to somewhere new, with desperate people as the excuse.

Is it too late to be a relief worker for CARE or Madre? Molly asked herself, and knew that it was. And then there was Paul, who would soon be back from Japan with a plan for them to go away together, to Ecuador perhaps. Her right eyelid began a slow flutter, as it sometimes did. "Fatigue or stress," the ophthalmologist had said on her last visit. "I suffer from neither," said Molly, but he did not answer, preferring not to banter with his uppity patients. She had never wanted to marry, but Paul, with his slight stammer and crooked smile, persuaded her that she was a deeply lonely woman who needed him. She had always thought that loneliness was embedded in every human being, sewn to the skin, stitched inside the brain. It was impossible to correct as if it were only high blood pressure or a jumpy heartbeat. She thought her father, who was so rarely alone, the loneliest of men, and perhaps Harry, despite the love of women, was too. She liked Paul so much that she did not resist his proposal.

"Just two more days," said Molly. "And I think your hair is growing back a little." Bertie looked pleased.

"I will go to see him alone," she said, but Bertie insisted on coming along, anxious to suture the rift.

Molly sat in the front seat with Ahmed, because Toby's girth and his tendency to sprawl made the backseat too crowded for the three of them and she loved watching Ahmed drive his old Citroën. At Tahar Djaout's house, they were surprised to be let in so quickly after ringing the bell only once as Bertie called out "Yoo-hoo" to announce that they were women. Toby was told to wait in the car, because the appearance of a man might startle the household.

"Oh yes, I am just the type recruited by the Groupe Islamique Armée," he said in a huff, hating to be left out of anything.

It was a thin man with a fine, nervous face who opened the door and pretended to have read the note they sent saying that they wished to see the writer. But he was not Tahar Djaout—he was his cousin. Tahar had gone to the office of his newspaper.

"His wife is not here. She has gone to the beauty salon, which may soon shut. The extremists have warned all hairdressers to close," the cousin said. "I am smoking too much, so I hope it doesn't bother you." After the door was bolted, they settled in large, stuffed armchairs in the living rooms, where the blinds were closed. The four large, ugly plants by the windows were drooping and dry. The windows were shut and locked. He crossed his legs, and one foot kept up a persistent and urgent jiggle.

"The maid has gone to a soothsayer to have her fortune told. Did you know there are five thousand of them registered in this country? This, too, is considered demonic by the Islamistes. So I am not able to offer you coffee. Tahar is very opposed to the Islamic factions and has written about them, but of course you know this."

"An American professor advised us," said Molly.

The cousin thought the visitors, with their pretty and intent faces, did not know what to ask him. The taller of them, with the more interesting, even haughty, face, showed him a copy of her book, saying she had so much wanted Tahar Djaout to sign it.

"Yes, the theme of it is interesting—how the obsession with the war against the French, and all our dead, made it so difficult for Algerians to go on living," said the cousin.

"Yes, we hear references to it even now," said Bertie. "But in our own country there are still many books on the Vietnam War. It has not been erased at all." The cousin smiled at her as if any comparison were invalid.

"I prefer Tahar's second novel, *Les Vigiles,* which came out in 1991 and is about the difficulties imposed on all Algerians by our officials," he said. "Of course, now he is too busy to continue writing novels." He lit a fourth cigarette.

He assumed they were with an American human rights group. It was his belief that Americans were always keen on that, but not so effective. Their government was too distrusted.

"We have a small plan," said Molly, hoping to stop the jiggling in his right ankle. She explained that she had with her some funds to provide those in danger with money for bodyguards, who could provide their own weapons. What did he think of this? She could only help a few, but that was better than nothing. She was not prepared to see him start laughing. He laughed so much that he had to fetch a glass of water from the kitchen to stop coughing, and it was a minute or two before he was his composed self and able to apologize. His cigarette smoldered in a glass ashtray.

"It is a great kindness on your part, and will you thank all those involved," he said, not guessing it was only Molly putting up the money. The bills still in her shoes felt slightly sodden, for it was a warm day.

"Here is the problem," he said, talking softly, as if he were sharing a secret. "There are too many to protect. Too many are in danger: journalists and writers and intellectuals, of course, but many, many others. Killing foreigners gives them more publicity, of course, and will lead to an exodus. It doesn't matter what they have done. And FIS is very clever. They know when and how to strike—"

There was a rough knocking at the door, and a man's voice called for him in Arabic. The startled cousin peered through the blinds and motioned for the women to scuttle into the kitchen. There were breakfast dishes still on the table and some rice in a pot on the stove. The cousin was trying to speak to the men through the door.

Bertie put her head down on the kitchen table, getting butter in her hair from the edge of a plate, and Molly was looking at a meat cleaver hanging on the wall and wondered if it was sharp enough to be a weapon. Perhaps a box of red pepper would be better. She expected the men might come storming inside the kitchen to kill them. In those terrible seconds, Molly, who dreamed when awake instead of in her sleep, saw herself sitting with Graham Greene, who lightly held her hand and said not to be afraid of the rat that was swinging on the faded curtain. "This is West Africa," Greene said. But she knew that: There was mosquito netting over a small bed. She grew peaceful looking at his long, elegant hand covering her own. He looked happy.

The cousin kept talking, the front door open, chatting with another man, who did not sound threatening. Surely if they meant to slaughter him it would be over quickly, but then the cousin called to the women to come out.

"It's all right. It was only the husband of the maid Leila, who had a friend drive him here. They don't have a telephone. She is not coming back to work after thirteen years. The fortune-teller said there would be blood everywhere outside the house and to stay away." Bertie, who believed in oracles, gave a sharp gasp.

He was not a superstitious man and tried to joke about it, but a zone of hope was now shrinking. Molly went upstairs to the bathroom to get some bills out of her shoes, and the rest out of her sports bra, wishing she had brought more with her. She inspected the bathroom, opening the medicine chest. She saw the sleeping pills, the hairbrush, some shaving cream, a deodorant, and a razor, but there was nothing that a woman might want. The cousin is living here alone, she thought. A woman would have done the breakfast dishes. She would have something of her own in the bathroom.

"This is our contribution," Molly said, handing over ten one-hundred-dollar bills. "I do hope you will consider protecting this house and the family. Perhaps a dog or watchman."

The cousin leaned over to kiss her hand. He had once seen a Frenchman do that outside the Crillon when he studied in Paris and always thought it an adorable ritual. Then he went to the large, dark desk, opened a secret drawer, and rolled the bills inside it. But there was no happiness on his face, and he was smoking again as they left.

Ahmed, a little troubled, had been circling the house for half an hour, with Toby napping in back, and saw the two men who had come to the door and leave, as did every woman who lived in the block and kept a lookout.

"I think that was Tahar Djaout, not his cousin," said Bertie. "He had the same eyeglasses I saw in the photograph on your book and the same—"

"Maybe so. He has to be careful," said Molly, thinking of the prophecy of the fortune-teller.

They went to the offices of the president of the Algerian Press Association. They talked to an editor at *El Watan*, who told them of a government communiqué with recommendations on security issues: "Banalize and minimize the psychological effect of terrorist and subversive actions. Play up atrocities committed by the Islamic regimes of Iran, Sudan, and Afghanistan." *La Nation* had been shut down for a week for trying to write about the government's human rights violation. A charming cartoonist showed them a drawing he had just finished of a reporter typing a story as a noose around his neck lifted him out of his chair.

A donation was made to the Algerian Press Association for the families of three reporters who had already been killed. Molly wished them well, Bertie said they would think of them, and Toby said something about grace under pressure, although it came out oddly in his French. It was the cartoonist who won their hearts with his eccentric humor and who had the last word. He called himself Zazi, a made-up name and perfect for this man, whose face was creased by his constant smiling.

"Mais, mes amis, il faut comprendre que nous sommes des condamnés." You must understand that we are the condemned.

All of them were bending under the strain, but Toby was carrying an extra burden of his own. The woman behind the curtain in the villa waited to see him come and go every day and blew kisses. He was ashamed of how deeply he feared and hated that creature and how she kept watch. He thought her face was turning redder and that perhaps she had some hideous skin disease, which would explain her isolation. It might be contagious.

"We must leave soon," said Bertie.

"Very shortly," added Molly.

A treat was being planned by Lucien, who felt it behooved him to do something nice for the visitors. They would go to the Casbah the following day to visit his friend Father André in his little school. It would surely please them to see the dear little children at their lessons. It was not a beguiling idea at all, but the three of them managed expressions of happy surprise, Toby being the least successful.

The trouble was that they had fixed ideas about the Casbah and dreaded going there. Toby had vivid thoughts of diseases, of bizarre germs not yet named by scientists, being spread by coughing and sneezing among people packed in so tightly. Bertie, who had weak ankles, feared the steep, narrow stone stairways and worried about how she would cover her hair. Molly, remembering the film *Battle of Algiers*, thought of the overhanging houses that almost touched, of the noise of the boots of the French paras, of secret passages and of many deaths, so much horror and triumph. She remembered reading that once the Casbah had been a haven for thieves, dope peddlers, and criminals, but it surely must have changed or Lucien would not take them there.

They set off with Ahmed, who did not look cheerful at the idea of such an excursion and declined to come with them. He would wait for their return on a nearby street. This might have been a signal, but Lucien's pleasure dropped over them like a veil of protective gauze, so they went ahead in a single file. The Casbah looked wrecked because of the huge gaping hole where reconstruction would begin, and it was poor Bertie, with her fear of them, who saw three busy rats. The old buildings were so close that anyone could jump from one rooftop to another. Passing one house with a black cavelike entrance, they saw a mirage: a light and large room in the rear with geraniums on a balcony. So it was not all squalor, but the smell of the Casbah was of very old, wet blankets to Molly, while Bertie would have said it was of rancid grease.

Toby, with his huge lungs, was not bothered by the climb and thought it funny that in the narrowest places he could almost touch buildings on each side with his outstretched arms. There was a humming of many lives, and the innocents marched on. It was only by chance that passing one house, its door ajar, Molly saw a huge chalk drawing on the wall of a boy's face with colored rays around the head, as if he had been beatified. It was an elaborate, loving, dreadful drawing, a memorial to young Ali La Pointe, hero of the Battle of Algiers, a freedom fighter but hardly a devout Muslim. Molly stepped into the room, thinking it was a public place, and it was a second before she saw that the peculiar shrine was presided over by a very young boy with such long curls and so pale a pallor that at first she thought him a Hasidic Jew. He stood behind a table that held leaflets in Arabic and could not believe his eyes.

"Is this the house where Ali La Pointe died?" she asked.

She looked for a plaque. "Leave," said the boy in Arabic, making a gesture at her to get out. The fact is that he had never seen a foreign woman and she was defiling the room. Outside, she asked Lucien where Ali La Pointe, the boy criminal recruited to fight the French, which he did with so much courage, had been killed, but Lucien shook his head and tried to hurry them on.

They were together in a very small square when all of them were caught and not clever enough to escape. Someone gave a piercing whistle twice, and five young men emerged from houses to encircle them. One grabbed Molly's bag, but she held on, kicking him so hard that he ran off, with only the strap in hand. Bertie ran back into the shrine to Ali La Pointe, child of these streets, and curled up under the table, holding on to the ankles of the appalled young Muslim who had never been touched by a woman except his mother. Toby was being punched and did not know how to defend himself. Nothing in his life—choirboy, seeing *The Guns of Navarone* five times, working at age sixteen as a Saturday boy in Bentalls department store, and the years of schooling—had prepared him for this moment. He was not quick on his feet and had always avoided sports, an indelible black mark against him. So he sat down and curled up, making him an easy target for the assailants, who began kicking him.

The attackers saw the small gold cross hanging on Lucien's neck. It was usually underneath his shirt, but was now in full view and easy enough to rip off. They held it up and shouted rich curses in Arabic. Lucien was trying to tweak their ears as an elderly schoolmaster might with pupils who were scrapping. But he hardly moved, believing it his sacred duty to take suffering upon himself, as Jesus had, rather than inflict it on others.

They were not boys of heft, but were scrawny, with the look of the preyed-upon as they went to work. Now they had found a calling, and the useless, wasted days were over, for older men had taken them in hand and their instructions were easy enough. It was their hope to go from the fist to the knife to the gun to the bomb.

Toby heard Lucien groan as one of his teeth was knocked out, and thought of his mother. Even as a child he had never been able to kick or run or jump, weighing far too much, and she had bought a badminton set to improve his co-ordination. "Come on, lambie," she would say as he lunged here and there.

Molly was hit in the face and disposed of quickly enough, so she stopped dancing around in her imitation of a boxer, yelling loudly for courage, ducking, and weaving, using the belt from her skirt to whip her accosters, who felt very little. Bertie was the safest, now running her hand under the trouser leg of the frozen, shocked fat boy. People came into the square, but only to watch. They found Molly entertaining before she collapsed. She urgently wanted to oppose the vicious boys, rather than just scream and crumple and bleed, as if something far greater were expected of her. All she was able to do was call up her dead father and what he had once told her when she confessed that she was scared of climbing the high rope in the school gym. It was required of all twelve-year-old girls, who would be tested the following Tuesday. He spoke to her gravely. "Find the fearlessness within yourself," he said. It was thrilling advice to the clumsy child, who asked if this was the way he had spoken to his troops during World War II, a wise and inspiring officer. It made him smile.

"Heavens, no," the father said. "They would not have liked such language at all."

Find it, find it, she told herself before she went down.

Toby, arms over his head for protection, curled up as tightly as he could manage, began to roll like a barrel after three or four savage kicks in his back. Down the steep steps he went until at last he came to a stop and moaned. The fun was over, and off went the attackers, who did not yet have the authority to kill, to their regret.

"I speak German perfect," Toby whispered when the others reached his side, remembering Gregory Peck's line in his favorite World War II film, since he now believed he had been wounded in a war. A woman, handsome and stout, frowning as if they had caused the ruckus, came out of her house with a glass of water for Toby. Bertie rummaged in her handbag, which had all sorts of useful things for those who expected to be taken prisoner, and found a painkiller called Roxicet, which she made him swallow. Lucien, bleeding from the mouth, ran to use the telephone in the school of Father André to call an ambulance; Toby's right arm looked very bad. Four men would be needed to lift him onto a stretcher. Molly swore to Lucien that there would be huge tips for each man, and he was to say this. Her mouth was split and her face hurt. Bertie gave her an aspirin, and she drank from the little glass. It was white with blue flowers, for brushing teeth she thought, and they returned it with profuse thanks to the woman with untidy black hair who stood there waiting to get it back.

The sun was shifting, so Toby, lying on hard ground, suddenly felt cold and began to babble, because the sound of his own voice seemed wondrous to him.

"I had a picture of Rommel on my bedroom wall for so many years that my little sister, Florie, thought he was English," Toby said. "All my friends and I were fascinated by the war, and especially the Germans, which worried my parents. They had a quiet word and said: 'Really, it isn't nice to be so interested in the German army.' My toys were model airplanes—Spitfires, Hurricanes, Mosquitoes. When I was six or seven, I assumed I would have to fight the Germans."

"It's all right, Toby," said Bertie. "Help is on the way."

It was worse when he fell silent again, for the women held the mistaken idea that if he did not talk, he might die, but Toby could not reminisce anymore. Lucien came galloping back to say that help was coming, and to their surprise it did. Toby was put on a stretcher, an old khaki one with a faint bloodstain already on it and two small rips, and the procession began. There was no way to strap Toby in, so Molly and Lucien had to hold on to him while Bertie led the way as they descended inch by inch and found Ahmed, who went into shock seeing Lucien holding his jaw, Molly with blood on her face, and Toby dead, which is what the driver assumed, for his face was chalky and he lay so still.

"Mum and I . . ." Toby began, and then rolled his head to one side, the fog closing in, the painkiller at work.

"A humeral fracture of the right arm with radial nerve damage," said the doctor, an Algerian who had done his studies in Lyons and was very good at reading X rays, even if they were of lamentable quality. "No cast, but he must keep the arm immobile in a sling." He showed them how: the arm bent and raised with the hand over the heart, in the way civilians gave a salute. "He will need a great deal of physical therapy if he is to use the arm again." He spoke slowly, as if to children, for they could not follow medical terms and he wanted to fend off too many questions, as doctors do. Lucien felt obliged to write it down so a clearer idea might be gained of whether poor Toby was permanently injured. A nurse cleaned Molly's mouth—no stitches needed—and looked at Lucien, whose teeth alarmed her. To the dentist, she said, and right away. But he had heard all that before and intended to have all his teeth pulled out anyway and wear dentures. He was sickened that he had led the others into the Casbah and had resorted to violence himself by pulling ears. His elbows were bruised from his being knocked down and a rib hurt when he breathed, but it was a small penance to pay. The loss of the cross was his great sadness.

"The monsters," said Eugène, tears in his eyes. "Wolves." He looked to Lucien to be steadied and was given a wan smile. Molly said he must not agitate himself—her French was now hardly understandable; sentences came out like broken pieces of an old plate—for she and Bertie were unharmed and would the following week make arrangements to take Toby to London and return to America, making it seem as if they were at fault.

But Toby was slow to recover. Bertie's Roxicet was all gone, and the hospital could not provide much pain medication. He was peevish and hated his bed, with its scratchy sheets, and wanted his mother. He ran a low fever. A sling had been improvised for the bad arm and he was told not to move. The doctor was anxious that he return to London but did not make this too apparent.

"If the bones are in union, he will not need a plate in his arm," he said. "The fever may be from a slight swelling in the brain." Surgery should be done in London, he added, as if they would consider anything else.

Molly and Bertie took turns reading to Toby from the one suitable book they had brought with them, *Nineteen Stories*, by Graham Greene, and because his favorite was "The Basement Room," they read it twice. " 'When the front door had shut the two of them out and the butler Baines had turned back into the dark and heavy hall, Philip began to live,' " read Molly, who loved that first sentence. The story was thirty-two pages long, so they read very slowly, and Toby's eyes misted when they came to the end, for he was deeply moved by the ruin of Baines and the little boy, who had so loved and trusted him but did not understand what Baines needed him to do. It was to lie.

So the three of them were alone again but did not speak of what Lucien had made known that morning: He had been obliged to file a report with the police, and two young men had been identified by a woman in the Casbah, who swore she saw everything. They were under arrest.

Molly began to read once more to Toby from a story she had already begun, "The Lottery Ticket," in the Graham Greene collection. Mr. Thriplow wins the jackpot after buying his first and last lottery ticket in Vera Cruz, a desolate little town in Mexico where he is on vacation. He donates the money to the governor to be used for good works, only to see shocking results and swifter persecution. As she read in her clear, low voice, her diction excellent for an American, Toby felt as if he were an indulged small boy and all that he lacked was a very hot cup of cocoa. Molly at last came to the end, and he made her read the final wrenching paragraph twice.

" 'It seemed to Mr. Thriplow, treading in his disappointed exile beside the sour river, that it was the whole condition of human life that he had begun to hate. A phrase came back to him out of his childhood about one who had so loved the world, and leaning against a wall Mr. Thriplow wept. A passer-by, mistaking him for a fellow-countryman, addressed him in Spanish.' "

She closed the little book with its worn, dark covers. Toby's face was wet, and he wiped his tears with the sheet and looked miserable. The story wounded him. He did not want to be a Mr. Thriplow, that poor fool.

"I suppose the two young men are being tortured even now," he mumbled. His nose was running, so Bertie wiped it with tissues from her bag. He seemed too tired to use his good arm to do this himself, and went on leaking.

It was easy enough for the journalist to find them in Toby's cheerless room, where he lay by himself, and he peeked in just as Molly was starting a new story. They thought he was with the hospital, but the young man gave each of them his calling card: HADI HASSI, JOURNALIST.

"I am a stringer for Agence France-Presse and some American publications," he said in excellent English, learned in a Jesuit school in Jordan, where his late father had had a business.

"You have had a very bad time," said Hadi Hassi. "May I have some details of your ordeal? Do you know who is to blame?" He was still new at the business and quite sheltered and did not realize that the different factions of FIS did not identify themselves with badges or slogans. Toby, who had never given an interview, rallied and tried to prop himself up on his one pillow. Bertie tried to help without jiggling the sling.

"We are very well aware of the extreme disarray that the country is in and why people might support FIS because of their government. Such allegiance is after all a form of opposition where no other expression of dissent is really possible," Toby began, but tired soon enough. He delivered a few more paragraphs until the pain had its way and silenced him. But he rallied for a little while.

"There is extreme hostility to foreigners, and I wonder why it is that we were not killed then and there on the spot as this campaign is clearly beginning," Toby said.

Hadi Hassi knew why, hesitated, and then shared his information.

"There are, as I understand it, sub rosa instructions to steer clear of Americans, not to hurt them. You might say they have a certain degree of immunity," Hassi said. "It is rumored that Washington has made contact with the so-called moderates in FIS so that they might go on talking, and while this is possible, there must be no attacks on Americans. Anyway, most of them will eventually leave. It is the other foreigners who are in danger, especially the French, who are seen as the enemy for aiding the government."

He was quite pleased with the effect this information had on Molly and Bertie, while Toby was indifferent. They looked with fierce suspicion at poor Hadi, as if it were not his business to know such things. Molly, eager to go on record, spoke out, standing against the wall, since there were not enough chairs for all of them and Hadi had to be seated to take his careful notes.

"We wished we might have talked to those young men in the Casbah who saw us as enemies, for we are not without sympathy for them—they are victims of their own wretched government and of abysmal poverty and hopelessness," she said. "We understand that if the Islamistes get into power, there will be no more elections, but they have already been robbed of a victory at the polls, so why should they believe in the democratic process? We extend our forgiveness to those who tried to hurt us, and I am sure I speak for Toby too."

Toby, who wanted to snooze, said: "Certainly."

After noting some details about Toby's arm and where Bertie had sought refuge, Hadi walked down the hall with her, his pen still out of his pocket and the notebook still open. Now he had only to hear her out.

"She is not herself at all. She is deeply concerned about the Algerian writers and journalists who are in danger. At home she is a very effective philanthropist, dispensing her own wealth to help others," Bertie said. "Her brother, Harry Benson, was slain in El Salvador in 1981. She has a great respect for journalists who take risks to report the truth."

Bertie took one wrong turn after another in this little summary and gave Hadi the hope that it might be a far more important story than he had guessed, at least 350 words for *The New York Times* and *The Observer* in London, if it happened to be a slow news day for both papers. It was. U.S. HEIRESS AND 2 OTHERS IN CASBAH ATTACK ran the headline in the *Times*, quoting Molly's every word. It was bad luck for her. Many, many people saw the story in the two papers and thought it a very foolish or disgusting comment.

A man from the British consular service came to see Toby in the hospital, and announced himself as L. M. Cathcart. He dryly mentioned a story in *The Observer*, suggested that no more be said about the Casbah incident, and offered to call his father in Epsom with details on Toby's flight home.

"Speak to him. My mum might go into a tizzy," said Toby, enjoying the chat with this fellow, for he was a bit weary of the company of the two American women. "It may have just been a robbery attempt. Someone tried to snatch Molly's bag before we were beat up. What do you think?"

"Time will tell," said L. M. Cathcart, arms folded, rocking on his heels, hating the smell of the disinfectant, which made his eyes water. He disliked any form of direct interrogation. Then, to his displeasure, Molly and Bertie came sweeping into the room, so he went on rocking on his heels, although, happily, they were not his concern.

"Is it true that the State Department has cut a deal with FIS's moderate factions that while they are talking to each other no Americans will be attacked?" asked Bertie. "This is what we've heard." It was always Bertie's technique to stand very close to a man when she wanted something, which Mr. Cathcart found brazen and unpleasant, because it unnerved him. Of course, he found her alluring in a coarse way.

"This information is quite unknown to us," he said, fleeing.

"Do you think we have been like Mr. Thriplow in the Graham Greene story, meaning so well and causing such grief?" Toby asked, looking at his feet sticking so far up under the sheet. Bertie said the idea was ridiculous, and even Molly, who partially believed it, shook her head. Her left cheek was badly bruised, but she did not care and would not let Bertie use her powdered rouge over her face to create a more healthy effect.

"The lottery money that Mr. Thriplow gave away was used to pay the wages of the police and soldiers, who then arrested the governor's opponent in the election," she said. "Really, Toby."

"But the two chaps who were picked up in the Casbah

might have been any young men and are now being tortured," said Toby, convinced they were all guilty of a considerable sin. They left him in a state of immense sadness, on his back as usual because of his arm, trying to pull the bedsheet over his face so he could hide. He wanted sleep. In this hospital, no one kept coming in to take blood or one's temperature. The sleeping just slept.

What the two women were unable to say to each other was precisely what Toby feared: that two innocent boys, taken at random, were in custody and suffering. The government forces were not merciful, and it wasn't in the least bit likely that a witness would have identified the real culprits, for retaliation would be very swift. Molly and Bertie, who knew so little, knew this much. "We must not dwell," was all Bertie said, but they would in the years ahead.

Now they went nowhere, unwilling even to let Ahmed drive them along the corniche. But it was dear Ahmed, on their last free day, who invited them for late morning coffee at his house, with its splendid view of the sea. His own father had simply moved in the day the French inhabitants left, taking one suitcase each. The woman was weeping. "Take down my name," she begged her husband, for the house, like so many others, bore a plaque: VILLA JACQUELINE. The villas were all named after the women who prevailed inside them. But there isn't time, the husband yelled at her, so the plaque with her name still hung outside.

The house was as spotless as Jacqueline had kept it, but the couches in the living room had been pushed against the wall, as Arabs prefer to do, so the living room looked bare.

The blue cushions were fading, and the little tables with the ornate lamps were too far away to be of use and two of them lacked bulbs. They sat in the dining room, Ahmed presiding proudly at the head of the table, which could seat ten, as his mother brought in thick black coffee in Jacqueline's old white demitasse cups. One of them was chipped, although she washed them lovingly. There were little cakes with odd pink icing, which only Toby devoured. Ahmed's mother, very fat and billowy in a long black skirt and loose red top, showed them pictures of her four daughters with their children, who looked exactly alike; Bertie and Molly paid the usual false compliments that plain children inspire. She made a fuss over Toby, who, because of his encased arm, seemed to tilt like an ocean liner and had difficulty sitting and rising on his first outing. She brought out a tiny jar of salve for Molly's cheek, with its yellow bruises. The salve was refused very nicely and put on the table by her cup.

"I will be sorry to see you go," said Ahmed, who chose not to mention that there had been a car bombing the night before, since it need not concern them. He thought they had been fine clients, and possibly the last to pay so well and to stay for so long. He still owed money on his car, and knew that his little brother was carrying that knife. Worry worked its way through him like a long inserted tube, going deeper every day.

Then Molly, with her pretty manners, agreed to try the salve, since it had been twice offered, and asked if there was a downstairs bathroom where she might apply some. It was down the hall, Ahmed said, under the staircase. There was a mirror. Toby was on his third cake with the pink icing.

At first she did not see Ahmed's brother creeping down the stairs. He looked like a hunted man in a strange place. He carried a small bag, not properly zipped shut, in which he had stuffed some clothes, including two of Ahmed's favorite T-shirts, which he had stolen. It was the day of his departure, an escape from Ahmed's questions and storms, his mother's whining inquisitions. He often stayed in the Casbah for days and then had to hear her plead that her heart would give out when the police finally came looking for him. The house was such an anxious place.

When the American and the boy first saw each other— he looking down at her, astonished—they instantly knew who the other was and what bound them. There were the little wounds, of course. On the boy's face was a crescent-shaped cut, on his right cheekbone, as if something metal had broken the skin. And it had. She had lashed him with her belt and the buckle did its work as he came at her. Although several inches shorter, he had inflicted a punch on her face, and the cut and the big bruise were proof of his power.

At first she hoped for a small sign of remorse, but he could not afford such a luxury. His work was cut out for him.

For a few seconds the combatants only stared at each other and stood very still in a frieze. And then Molly, unable to speak, did a peculiar thing, which she was to keep secret for the rest of her life, as if it were too mystifying to explain. She edged up the stairs to get closer to him, and although frightened that she might betray him to Ahmed, he remained silent and still. The boy could always sense a conspiracy of any kind. She wanted to ask who were the two boys arrested. Had they really been with him, or were they innocent? But she did not dare. Then she whispered to him, and the boy, two steps above, seemed to bend his head to hear, or so she imagined.

"I am so sorry for everything," Molly said in French, which he pretended not to understand, and she reached out lightly to touch his hand on the banister, a small benediction.

She hardly knew what she meant, sorry perhaps for what was happening to his country and for the boy's own ferocity. She did not believe him a murderer, and she could not resist his need for help. Her thoughts wobbled, but she believed it was not up to her to trap someone so desperate and so lost. She would not inform on him. She did not understand that the boy, with his sly eyes, felt happiness and pride at being recruited by FIS. He had never been invited to join anything until FIS wanted him.

Ahmed had once told them that his brother had done well at school and wanted to play the guitar and now he was just a thug in the Casbah. She remembered Saadi's face very clearly, and he hers, as they had briefly fought each other, and on the staircase they thought each other quite ugly. To him, she looked old and disgusting. Then Molly signaled to Saadi that there were guests—as if he could not hear the

voices, Toby and Ahmed laughing at something—and motioned for him to go back upstairs.

There was no light in the tiny bathroom in the hall and
the bare bulb looked black. She could not see her face. The
reddish salve that Ahmed's mother had bestowed smelled
like old mustard. It was so caked that she had to dig out
small slivers with a fingernail. It did not dissolve on the
skin. In the dining room, no one remarked on how peculiar
she looked, with bits of it sticking to the extravagant bruise.
Ahmed drove them home and plans were made to get them
to the airport the next day. He looked melancholy, so they
found themselves lying to him, their voices too high-
pitched and exuberant.

"When the turbulence is over, we will come back," said
Bertie. "We will all go together to see the ruins at Tisala."

"And to the Sahara," said Toby, frantically. Molly was
quiet.

While they were in the car, Ahmed's brother heard his
mother in the kitchen washing the cups and plates, humming to herself, and he set out again, tempted to kiss her
good-bye yet despising himself for such sentimentality. He
thought he might never see the house again, and left for
his war.

I t was Toby who gave Molly away, and felt not the smallest
bit of remorse. That day at Ahmed's house, he had risen to
go to the toilet and just made it to the doorway when he saw
Molly whispering on the stairs to that dreadful boy from the

Casbah, who had kicked him in the ribs when he was down. He lumbered back to the table, telling the others that he felt a bit dizzy and should sit for a while.

"I must go to the police and tell them that we can identify our attackers. We saw them at close range. The boys they are holding will be let go. We can say, once and for all, that those chaps are innocent," Toby said, talking to himself. He did not want their detention on his conscience and swore that the mess must be cleared up as soon as possible.

"Father," Toby began, as he cornered Lucien just as the diligent man was beginning to chop up vegetables for dinner by the kitchen sink. He knew Lucien was not a priest but still preferred to start his entreaty this way. It was fitting for a supplicant.

"I need to talk to you about Molly. She has done some dreadful things. She has talked to one of the boys who hurt us in the Casbah and then said nothing. He was the one who kicked me—I shan't forget his face soon. He should be arrested."

Lucien led him to a chair and helped Toby lower himself, like a vast broken umbrella. Toby's voice was growing stronger, as though he were making a speech in a crowded room and needed to be heard by those dozing in the back row.

"You and I must go to the police and give them the address of the guilty boy. It is Ahmed's villa. I hope you won't recommend him as a driver in the future. He has a dangerous family."

Lucien felt alarm like a dull pain circling in the stomach before it settled on a certain point. It was the worst possible time to draw attention to the house. He saw the dark raisin eyes of the policemen, the endless papers to be filled out, the questions that might go beyond that unhappy day in the Casbah. How he could possibly explain what the foreigners under his roof were up to, since he did not know himself? When he had first reported the attack, he skimmed over such details, but now all this information would be required, or demanded, of him.

"Molly has given money to FIS, to a lawyer who works for them. Did you know that, Father?" Toby said. "She has simple and dangerous ideas. Like many Americans. As you know, I have been living in that country."

Staring at Lucien, he saw nothing in his face that gave him hope for a small measure of justice. He is a coward, Toby thought, a disgrace to the church. Here comes the little smile to calm me. It did not occur to Toby that the police were too busy to worry about that day in the Casbah, that much else was going on, that the morgues were filling up, the dossiers rising in careless piles, and that, above all, they did not want to be pestered.

"You must be calm, and I will think about all this and what is the best thing to do," said Lucien. He wanted to be at ease again and not have to pass judgment, and he knew this was weakness on his part. Molly seemed a pleasant and peaceful woman, and the idea of her giving money to FIS, as Toby claimed, was unlikely. Perhaps he is affected by those pills he takes at night so he can sleep, Lucien thought. Pain can do strange things to the mind.

Upstairs, Molly was writing a short letter to her husband in Osaka, the last one from Algeria, which she hoped Ahmed would mail. She was complaining about Toby. "He is growing most peculiar and it is surely because of his poor arm. This morning he told me he had to live by Christian beliefs regardless of what others did. It was astonishing.

"I want to be able to trust people, but this is so often a mistake," Molly wrote. "We leave tomorrow."

What she wrote to Paul hardly did justice to the encounter with Toby. Emotion streamed out of him; he might have been a furnace overheating the room. He refused to sit down, as if such an indulgence might compromise the courage of a staunch man and muddle his explanations of the correct responsibilities of a Christian.

"Surely this makes sense to you," Toby said. "After all, Graham Greene was a Catholic writer."

"He hated being called that," Molly said. "He was a writer who happened to be Catholic. Only three—no, four, I think—of his novels reflect that. His characters have faith or half faith or huge doubts or no belief. It is his compassion for the poor and the tormented and the lonely that is so haunting. He once said that he liked old communists at the moment when they were losing their faith."

Oh God, Toby thought. How she does go on. And she only spent a few hours with the great man. Molly's eyes were closed, as if a sudden spasm of exhaustion required this. She gave a long sigh.

It was at this moment that Toby disowned her.

He began his note to the police in block letters, saying that a criminal who was hunting foreigners lived at this address in Algiers and had already wounded some on this date in the Casbah. There were two suspects in jail who were probably innocent. It was the duty of the police to get the guilty boy. It took him three tries to write a clear, concise message. In French he slid and splattered, no matter the effort. He had not the slightest idea of how to deliver his note, for the walk to the police station in place Allende required more energy than he could summon. Toby went to sit outside in the orange deck chair when he saw Eugène's pupil Dalila leaving the house.

"I have something to ask you," said Toby.

"Bonjour," she said, in slight reproach for his abrupt manner. They went outside, with Toby listing badly— writing the note had worn him out—so she opened the heavy wooden door.

"Will you take this to the police station for me?" said Toby. She looked at him blankly. I'm not asking her to take off her clothes, Toby thought, a short fuse of fury beginning to burn. He was starting to hate all foreigners. Does she want to be paid? he wondered. Molly had given him cash at the start of their trip in case they were separated, and he thought she would not expect to get it back.

"This is for your trouble," he said, handing her two ten-dollar bills. She pretended not to understand his French and required him to repeat everything twice, which he did, in his desperation, so she would stop saying, *"Quoi? Quoi?"* A more confident and cunning man might have kept her there to make his case and impress upon her the seriousness of the little errand. Dalila looked at the bills—she had never seen American money before—but they were without importance, for she did not know their value.

It took her another week to complete the little mission for Toby, and she taped the bills to a mirror in her bedroom, because they were so green and exotic. Toby's note was opened at the police station, and one man, who read it, said: "It's a prank written by a schoolboy." But he did not throw it out. It lay in a box for some time, until someone else thought it required a visit to the house of Ahmed Hocine.

After their last dinner—Lucien made a stew with meat and a few too many onions—Molly waited for the others to go to bed so she could speak her mind. She held an idea that Lucien must be told how much she admired him for his being willing to hide an Algerian family at such risk to himself. This was her last chance. She believed people deserved praise when they showed exceptional courage, even if she was not the one to do it.

"You are a brave man, and I wish you well in the days ahead," said Molly. It startled him, and with reason, for he had done nothing unusual except offer the guest rooms to his friend Ali, whose house was so crowded with eleven of his children, his mother, and an aunt. It was Ali who had asked Lucien for help: His seven-year-old son had suffered a compound fracture of the leg and was in a long cast for eight weeks. There was no place for the child to lie down, since he shared his little bed with a younger brother, who kicked in his sleep, and the living room always seemed jammed with people. Ali often forgot the names and ages of his own offspring, so crowded were their quarters. It was thought that the injured child might benefit from peace and quiet, and would be sent over with his grandmother, who would stay with him and prepare the child's food. It did not occur to Lucien to tell Molly about this, so she was always to believe that the heroic man was hiding fugitives— from death squads, Molly thought, another country coming to mind.

"It is so good of you to help people who are desperate," said Molly, not guessing that praise made him deeply uncomfortable unless it was a word or two from the venerable French cardinal. That always came when Lucien and Eugène went to see him, in the huge mansion that was still his realm, and the cardinal remembered it was he who had attached them to each other.

"All of us have a duty to help the distressed," said Lucien. "And I do very little."

She thought it a lovely lie and put her hand on his shoulder as if they were soldiers in an undeclared struggle. She did not notice that he drew back a little, unaccustomed to the touch of another person.

"You must get some sleep," said Lucien, anxious for her to leave so that he could undress, say his prayers, and go to sleep on the battered sofa; the company of other people suddenly seemed punishing. He was beginning to miss the old days when there was only Eugène and the calm in their lives had held a blessed monotony. But Molly was not done and had one more thing to tell him.

"The other day, someone came in our rooms and went through my things and Bertie's," she said. "Nothing was taken. Perhaps the door downstairs should be locked all the time."

If she had struck him, he would not have been more astonished, and said nothing. Both of them simply waited to be released. It was up to him to speak.

"Perhaps Eugène was looking for the sewing kit, which is kept on the shelf in your armoire," Lucien said, unable to do better than this. He sat down on the couch and began slowly to take off his shoes and socks so Molly would leave him alone.

The last day left Molly and Bertie stricken. As the car was being loaded with luggage outside the compound, Lucien carrying Toby's knapsack, there was a sudden hoarse shriek from the villa outside the gate. It was Toby who first saw the vile old Frenchwoman leaning out the window. She pulled down the silly curtains so they covered her head and shoulders like a dingy veil. "Wait, wait," she screamed, and then threw down a note, already written in block letters and badly creased, as if it had been done years ago. It said: "Take me with you. I have a cousin in Nantes." The woman leaned out the window, lifting her long, very white, thin arms in a final plea before someone yanked her away. It was Lucien, after retrieving the note, which landed in a bush, who quietly said: "There is the question of a passport, an exit visa, and whether her cousin is still alive." Toby thought he might faint. Ahmed said, "Don't interfere. Let's go." Molly and Bertie kept staring at the window; there were noises of a quarrel inside the house and a man shouting in Arabic. The women felt their hearts knocking. It was hardly possible to get inside the car, except, for the first time, they saw Ahmed becoming angry. You will miss your flight, he warned. No one had ever begged for help before Molly's eyes in such a wild, beseeching way, but she did nothing and felt only a leaden sense of resignation. The woman, out of sight, gave a last useless cry.

Molly left the rest of her money with Lucien, to be used for the poor or the families of the slain, or whatever he pleased. It worried her slightly that Lucien seemed aloof, but he had begun to brood about Toby's accusations and feared that Molly may have been tricked into giving FIS money and that there might be dire consequences if this ever came to light. Lucien saw that the tic in Molly's eye was beginning its strange little jig as they parted, and he resolved to pray for her. There was a huge tip for Ahmed, which would keep him going for another year, and he felt giddy stuffing it in a pocket.

So they were off, and in his happiness Toby began to sing, although softly, since the women were unraveling. It was one of the hymns he loved. "Thine be the glory," sang the old choirboy, "risen conquering sun . . ." Molly thought it was an Easter hymn, with music by Handel, and that it was tasteless of Toby to show off at such a mournful time.

At the airport, only Ahmed maintained his dignity as Bertie and Molly clung to him. Molly knew it was the last time they would have his protection and guidance.

"Come to the United States," she blurted out. "I will get you a job and a place to live." Ahmed patted her shoulder while shaking his head. It was Bertie who went too far as she began kissing his face and not stopping when she reached his mouth. When kissing the plump face of her husband, Bertie was reminded of scented fruit, a plum perhaps, slightly past its prime. But this man's face felt like rope and bone, which she found thrilling. Ahmed had one arm around Bertie's waist, because she was leaning into him as she began to kiss his lips. Molly tugged her away. People were staring. Among the onlookers was the Reuters man, without hand luggage, wondering what was going on with these women.

"Write us," said Molly.

"You must," said Bertie in a delirium. "We will wait for word." They waved and sniffled and marched forward.

But there was no word. Weeks went by and nothing came from Algiers. Molly always worried about important mail, feeling she had been horribly betrayed by the post office. The last letter she sent to Graham Greene in Corseaux, not knowing he was hospitalized by then, was returned to her weeks after his death. It lacked five cents postage. "Five cents," she cried out, holding up her last letter to the writer, with all the love it carried. Elsie was now ordered to put at least twenty cents' additional postage on all letters to Algiers as a precaution. Nothing could be taken for granted.

Five letters, with extra postage, were sent to Ahmed in Algiers, yet nothing came back, and she began to fear he was dead until word finally came. He did not tell her that he had been arrested when the police came looking for his brother, at last ordered to act on Toby's note. But it had not gone too badly for him in six days of confinement, except for insane hunger. He remembered Molly with something close to tenderness, although he would not have called it that. In his entire life no one had ever offered him help as she had, her thin hand holding out the money bunched under a green rubber band. And he remembered her running to reach the two men being dragged by the police. He had never seen a woman run like that. He did not know how to put any of this into words, and did not think it useful. Ahmed wrote on a piece of graph paper, and she had trouble reading it, but there were only a few lines: "Don't write. It goes badly for us. I am under suspicion because I claimed my brother's corpse. He wanted to be important and has put the family in danger. My mother is ill."

The letter had been mailed from Paris; perhaps a friend or client had done him that favor. And then the dying really began, by the gun or the bomb. The president of the ruling Supreme State Council was shot and killed in June, five months after a bloodless military coup. Toby called

Molly from England, Molly called Toby, and all their conversations were about casualties. It was his new silky manner that made her suspicious. It suggested a degree of treachery on his part, but she could not guess the consequences: Ahmed in an old French prison without bed or toilet or running water for six days, Lucien believing that she had been duped into giving money to the extremists. It was dangerous to know too much, and she feared personal quarrels. I have been mistaken so many times, Molly thought. But at least I have not stood aside, eyes shut, and been a coward. The very word made her smile. It was Graham Greene who quoted Robert Louis Stevenson to her: " 'Envy me, envy me, I am a coward . . .' " He was explaining why nothing would induce him to spend even a few hours in El Salvador during its war but the younger Greene had been reckless and unflinching so many times.

When President Boudiaf, a hero of the war of independence, was shot in the back and in the head while giving a speech, Molly read Toby the last words he spoke: " 'We must know that the life of a human being is very short. We are all going to die. Why should we cling so much to power' . . ."

They could hardly keep count of the slain: nuns and priests and Trappist monks, journalists and writers and editors, businessmen, teachers, and students, women who were covered and women who were not, villagers going about their daily lives or sleeping. Hadi Hassi bled to death in an explosion, Toby reported, for *The Observer* had carried a small notice. Father André, whom Lucien once wanted them to meet, was shot to death in front of children. The cartoonist, Zazi, was also gunned down.

The militant groups had pulled apart, and the most ruthless among them killed four Catholic priests outside of Algiers in a reprisal for the deaths of four of its members in the hijacking of a flight to Marseille. Statements were faxed to news organizations saying that the priests were killed as part of a campaign of "annihilation and physical liquidation of Christian crusaders." Molly knew Lucien could face his death most bravely, but it would go so badly for Eugène, who would need to hold his friend's hand, if there was time.

She telephoned Lucien at home in Algiers to implore him to leave and return to France, where he could work with impoverished communities of Algerians. He said very little on the telephone, and his tone of voice was neutral, not pleased. Eugène's headaches were worse and both of them stayed indoors. He no longer even went to the hospital. She guessed that the Algerian family was still hiding in the house. Friends came with food, Lucien said.

"Then you put them in danger," Molly said, who grew impatient with piety. She pitched a last entreaty at him.

"God will tell us what to do," Lucien said, and added that he was so happy that Toby was recovering use of his injured arm and that he had prayed for this. And then the benediction: "We believe that dawn is on its way."

It was too perilous for journalists in Algeria, so there

were only occasional stories from local stringers or correspondents who could pass as Arabs. Once on television she saw the "ninjas"—the government's special hit teams, who wore black masks over their faces—rounding up some men who looked terrified. One of them resembled the doctor in the hospital who told the madman to wring the mop.

"If they had not been cheated of that election by the generals, none of this might be happening," Toby said from London. "But the fundamentalists will lose their support if the killing goes on. People will hate them more than the government, or just as much."

It was Bertie, the early riser, who first read the little obituary in *The New York Times* for Tahar Djaout but waited until 9 A.M. to call Molly. She dreaded the call, believing that Molly had suffered a cave-in she could not begin to describe, a sort of collapse at the core. Molly was teetering. The Algerian writer had been shot in the head as he left his house in the morning, his wife watching him go from the window. He was thirty-nine years old and lived in Bainem, nine miles west of Algiers. Only then did Molly understand that it really was his cousin who had received them and that they had gone to the wrong address. Or that it was not his cousin at all. She was never to know the answer, and the uncertainty grated on her.

Sometimes she thought of Ahmed's brother and that thin, tense face with its intaglio of grim duty and his murderous dreams. There was the suspicion, too, that he had helped kill Tahar Djaout, and while there was hardly a reason to believe this, she did, as if in a delirium. She had never been so certain of anything and there was no one to say: You are wrong; other men did the job.

She sent a check in French francs to Tahar Djaout's publisher in Paris, asking them to forward it to his wife. Most of all, she wanted his novels to be translated into English and published in New York and London, but there was no interest at all in the publishing houses she wrote to, and sometimes not even the courtesy of a reply. Strings were pulled and snapped. Even, at long last, when she was together with her husband, Paul, who had finally finished his Japanese film and had recovered from his infatuation with the Japanese film editor, Molly kept trying. She knew that Graham Greene would have helped—he had done so much for other writers who needed recognition and deserved praise. There was no one now to honor the Algerian killed in front of a tidy house, walking quickly to start his day. Toby tried, Bertie tried, although they knew it to be hopeless. And the death tolls in Algeria kept rising, up and up. Americans were not interested; the White House was silent. Oh those Arabs, Mrs. Benson would say.

"It was a waste of time our going there, wasn't it?" said Molly on the telephone to Toby.

"Oh no. I've written a short paper for a small academic journal, which I will send to you," Toby said. She found it an offensive reply and was silent, so he spoke up. His ruined arm gave him authority.

"You helped as best you could with your donations. Think of that. The point is that there doesn't seem to be very much that we could have done."

"We couldn't even save Tahar Djaout," she said.

"He needed a dog, or a bodyguard. You wanted that for him." She was not to be consoled.

Toby, happy to be back in England and recovering nicely from surgery on his arm, was not conscientious about doing the exercises the physical therapist at the hospital had ordered. Fiona was coaxing him to open his hand, then make a fist, so that the tendons in his wrist would not stiffen as the radial nerve in the arm recovered. One hundred and fifty times a day, the physical therapist said sternly, for she never trusted patients.

"Why did you send a note to the police? You might have talked to your driver about what his own brother had done in the Casbah," said Fiona. Twice she had heard the dreary story, but thought Toby needed to march through it again if he was ever to regain his equilibrium.

"He was probably in on it," said Toby, recklessly. "After all, he refused to come into the Casbah with us. Now I see why. There was no one I could turn to. It's shocking that Molly did not want to see such a wicked boy properly punished after what I endured."

"But Molly sounds like a good person," said Fiona, watching Toby's huge hand open and shut and keeping count.

"Oh yes, but it wasn't she who suffered, was it?" said Toby. "People like her never do. They just take a stand while the bullets hit someone else."

olly was losing her apartment as the little building on Nassau Street was sold and her lease was up. She knew it was hopeless finding another one for a low rent that was so handy to everything. The odd little apartment, where so much and so little had happened, had never seemed important until now, when she began to love it. It stood, as she never suspected, for safety. The furniture and boxes of files would be stored in the house on Lilac Lane, with its vast, clean cellar. But the letters from Graham Greene in the white folder and three years of checkbooks, office-size, would be carried by hand and kept in a drawer in the bedroom that she and Paul would now pretend was their own until future plans were clear.

Molly made the mistake of sitting down with the folder and going through the letters. For the first time, she saw how weak and pathetic her claim on him was, how the letters had bestowed an importance she inflated beyond reason, and that, worst of all, she might have been a nuisance to him. Because of the clippings she sent, year in year out, the kind man had always answered. A niece did the typing now, for his sister was ill. Letters always ended "Affectionately, Graham."

There was the new stationery with the Corseaux address and she missed seeing *La Résidence des Fleurs* on the letterhead, the fanciful name for the little apartment house in Antibes where he lived in rooms without distinction except when he was in them. It was here, in the living room, where they had once sat in chairs watching the evening news on French television. This was his habit. She could not remember what was being reported, in her happiness, while he was attentive and grumbled that the coverage was never very good.

In the last of the letters, two months before his death, to acknowledge an article on dreams, he held fast to his theory that dreams took incidents from the future as well as the past. "The other interesting point is that it's the dreams which refresh and not the sleep," he wrote. And then the final single sentence, which fell with a huge thud: "I'm in the same state of bad health which is likely to continue to the bitter end." The letter was slightly crumpled; she had clutched it to her chest.

In her own living room, windows smeared by slanting rain, it came upon her that she had arrived at a bitter end of her own, and saw there were no important possibilities ahead. Molly had seen the absurdity of her life before, that was nothing new, but now there was no reason to ever believe in her own usefulness again, and it was this pretense which she so needed. Algeria had banished all hope. She was sitting perfectly still, the cherished letters still in her lap, when her mother called to say dinner would be at seven-thirty and Posy Stretch would join them, anxious to hear about the trip.

Around her were the achievements of Graham Greene,

lying in boxes closed by strips of silver duct tape, which, since her eyes were watering from dust, appeared to be large blurred crosses. Buried were the novels, the nonfiction, the plays, the film reviews, the essays and articles, the book reviews, and his letters to the press in a green volume called *Yours etc.* Buried were the memoirs in which he had taken such care not to betray or diminish people he had once loved. She knew that no such mercy would be granted him and, now that he was dead, that malevolent and jealous people would write about him, as would those who were simply craven. She hoped to harden her heart as she once had when hearing, in a snazzy hotel in San Salvador, that Harry embellished his stories from Central America. She knew how to do this.

And then, as if a letter from him might provide a push to go on with her daily life, as if courage could be swallowed from a sheet of paper, she read one of his letters at random. It was only four years old. He sounded very pleased and unquestionably surprised by a review she had sent from *The Washington Post* of *The Captain and the Enemy,* his newest book. It was by Leon Edel, the biographer of Henry James, whom he considered one of the best literary critics in both their countries. "I have all his editions of Henry James on my shelf. To be reviewed by him was an honour and I never expected him to be a favourable reviewer," he wrote. And then the usual bit of news: He had been to Russia last year for his birthday and had had to blow out eighty-four candles! Good-bye, good-bye now, she whispered, and shoved off.

What was left undone was to honor the murdered Algerian novelist, as if his books might make clear why his country was now in ruins, its promise throttled as its citizens slaughtered each other with ardor. No one seemed to understand her insistence on this. It will blow over, a few friends said, look at Lebanon. It was only when she thought of publishing the novels herself in a series, perhaps, of Third World writers, a project Graham Greene might have blessed, that her husband interfered. Always so tolerant of her projects, he felt she must give up the idea, for it was futile. He had never seen her weep before until he spoke his mind as they stood in her mother's garden near the forsythia bushes, Molly leaning against a tree, her face close to the bark. He did not understand what the trouble was. She was always so steadfast and undaunted. It was what he most loved about her.